SLEEPLESS
BEAUTIES

THE VAMPIRE'S VENDETTA

SLEEPLESS BEAUTIES

USA TODAY BESTSELLING AUTHOR

A.K. KOONCE

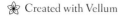

For anyone who's ever accidentally found love.
And rejected that shit immediately.

CONTENTS

ONE

Kira

The man across the street drags his chair closer to his date as they eat their brunch like they invented love and lust and...

Well, cheating.

"Oh Robert, Robert, Robert..." I whisper as I snap another quick picture from behind the lamppost I'm leaning into.

His hand drags up her thigh, shoving at the yellow sun dress she wore for him. My phone rings and I nearly drop the thing in a rush to get my picture before...

Noooo! Gah just let it fall next time, Kira!

Shit.

Right now? We're doing this right now?

"Yeah? Hey! Hi, Mom," I say into the phone while I try to get a shot of the woman fondling Robert's dick from over his gray slacks. "No, now's not a bad time. It's fine." I snap another ten or so of a far too up-close picture of the elderly man's cock.

My gag reflex sounds just as my mom asks if I'm still dating Chad.

"Oh, stop. He's a nice young man, Kira. Your sister would have loved him."

This time my grimace has nothing to do with life alert hand jobs and everything to do with the current conversation.

"Kyra would have agreed," I whisper quietly.

"Come home for Thanksgiving?" she asks in that way that only mothers do. It's that I'm asking, but there's really no question mark tagged at the end of that demand.

"Of course, Mom." I glance at the time and if I don't ditch Robert's daylight dick play and my mother's phone call right now, I'm going to be late. "I got to go, Mom."

A pause drifts across us like it always does.

"Love you," I add, and I know she'll say it back. And I'll hang up first. And she'll call again. Same time, same day next week.

The call ends, and I swipe quickly through my phone to email over all the pictures to Robert's sweet darling wife who will use them to get all the alimony he can afford.

With that job done, I'm officially off work for the weekend.

But I have one more thing to do before I go home. I jog across town. If I don't hurry, I'll miss her. Again.

And then I won't be able to see her for another month.

The cold fall air bites at my cheeks as I turn the corner and stop dead on the crimson line painted into the old sidewalk. One side is newly paved. Long and unending, leading through a neighborhood my kind hasn't ventured into in over nine decades. It'll be an even ten at the end of this year.

As for the other side—my side—the pavement is cracked and worn. And that's because my side is Chicago tax dollar kept instead of Crimson City kept. It's just one more thing that shows how supernaturals care more about perfect appearances than humans do.

It's not something the average human thinks about.

What I wouldn't give to be average. Unknowing. Naïve.

Instead, I'm very well educated.

Unfortunately.

Because we're not alone on this earth. There truly are things that go bump in the night.

And one of those things is walking toward me right now.

"Hey, Pretty Human," the charming but arrogant vampire bows to me.

My lips curl at the way he always over familiarizes his nickname for me. He does it on purpose. He knows how much it makes my illogical heart stutter, and he rejoices every time.

That's why humans will always be weaker than vampires. It isn't their supernatural speed or their immortality. It's just humanity's foolish nature to think that just because something is *pretty* it should be *valued*. The man's flawless white smile and shimmering eyes are a case in point.

"Prey." His bizarre name is spoken flatly against my tongue. Carelessly. I want him to know that although he might make a shiver of uneasiness race across my body, he himself is nothing to me.

His tight fitted tee-shirt goes unnoticed, let me assure you. As does the way it rides up at the bottom, exposing lickable veering lines and just enough hair leading down the center of his hard stomach to make me choke on my own saliva like an old cat.

Completely. Un. Noticed.

Unkempt hair as dark as the night sky flits over his ice-cold eyes. A venomous sneer lingers in his gaze. The unnoticed shirt that hugs his lean frame is the same inky color of his locks, as are his jeans. And his boots, and probably even the arrogant underwear hugging his arrogant ass.

He's my sister's assistant... boyfriend? I don't actually know.

But every month, when I come here to the Crimson City line to see my sister, this asshole has always accompanied her.

Except for today.

Because this time he's alone.

"Where's Kyra? It's the sixth. Today's our day." The speculation in my tone can't be helped. It's something that has been ingrained into my very being. Doubt everything and everyone.

It comes from being paid to find out secrets. And everybody has at least one or two hidden away.

Mothers lie. Ministers cheat. And the boyfriend? He's always guilty. If you were to call me and the word boyfriend comes up, we both already know what I'm going to find.

Vampires, they can't be trusted at all. Not even a little bit.

This one's no different.

He blinks his violent blue eyes at me. They're pretty today, really. At least this time his eyes are not shadowed with the blood of his dinner lingering in his gaze.

They looked... gentle. And a little remorseful, if I didn't know any better.

His dirty black boots scrape against the pavement as he looks away from me. The red line between us is a glaring notation. He doesn't touch it.

Nor do I.

"Miss Vega cannot make it today. I've been advised to dismiss you this month." There's definitely something hidden behind those pretty prep-schoolboy eyes when he finally brings his attention back to me.

He can pretend to be proper and fake being polite,but we both know he isn't.

A beat passes in silence as I pick apart his words, his stance, his stare, his every minute detail.

Dark circles rim his inky lashes. His already lean frame has a more careless slouch today, if that's even possible. A tired sort of stance. And as for what he just said... No one knows that I meet my twin sister here on the sixth of every month. He didn't say Kyra asked him to send me an update, he said he had been advised...

By whom?

Who else could possibly know about me?

No one. Kyra wouldn't take that chance. She wouldn't dare tell anyone about her human sister.

Just like I wouldn't even tell our mother that Kyra didn't actually die two years ago. That she's alive and... Well... as close to alive as an undead monster can be anyway.

So the bigger question isn't who knows and who sent him, but...

"Why isn't she here?" I take a single step closer to the dangerous line that to the average eye would be overlooked. And because of the magical spell interwoven with that line, it would naturally be avoided by the more oblivious of my kind.

Lucky them.

Prey tilts his head to the side, a smug smirk cutting over his lips as he looks down on me. His hands slide into his pockets as if he's cold in the autumn weather but I know he feels nothing.

Not a damn thing.

"Careful, Pretty Human. You wouldn't want to cross that line."

My jaw grinds hard as I keep my mouth shut about the one thing I can never tell anyone. Especially his kind.

They'd kill me for it.

Because the humans who know about supernaturals, don't

step over into their world. And they've agreed not to come into ours.

My sister and I break this rule once a month. We don't dare to break the rule often.

I break it more than they'll ever know but that's my own little secret for just me to keep.

"I want to see her myself."

A car slows with squealing brakes as it travels down Crimson Road. Just as it nears the city line, the car comes to a full stop. The driver shakes his head. It takes him a minute to reevaluate whatever it is the magic shows him. A dead end? More endless road construction?

Whatever it is, he reverses because of it. He turns his little white sedan right around and will more than likely forget he ever drove down this cursed lane.

I wish I had.

Honestly, it would have been easier to believe Kyra had died that night on our eighteenth birthday. It was far easier than learning the twisted truth.

"I want to see her!" I state with an edge biting my tone.

I knew something would happen. I knew the moment she snuck directly into my apartment to confess her worst fears.

Those fears are clearly alive and well now.

"Did it ever occur to you that she doesn't return that sweet sentiment? Perhaps she has grown tired of keeping the stale relationship with her weak little sister alive." Everything he says is so condescending and cruel. It pains me not to throat punch him, just to cut into that obnoxiously proper tone of his a little.

I storm forward and maybe I will punch him. Maybe I'll tackle his scrawny ass to the ground and give him a kick for every single spiteful thing he's ever said to me over the last two years.

But I only make it one step.

My sneakers hit the red line and before I can lunge at him, he surprises me.

His shoulder slams into my stomach hard enough to knock the wind out of me. I tense for the impact of the sidewalk to crash against my back.

But the collision never comes.

With a fluid movement, he flings my entire body over his shoulder and strides down the Chicago sidewalk in broad daylight. It's a languid walk of complete casualness as I bring my knee to his chest over and over again, my nails claw into his back with every step he takes. Still, he just carries on as if there isn't a hundred and thirty pound rabid cat of a woman hissing obscenities right to his very taut ass. God, why is his ass the only thing I can see right now? His slim jeans hang just a little, and I notice that his underwear is black as well, just as I predicted. And his shirt keeps riding up. Are those dimples? He has back dimples?

Stop making my heart stupid!

"Put me down!"

A sparking flick of sound strikes, then I hear him inhale deeply.

Is... is he having a smoke right now?

"No can do, Vega."

The scent of nicotine hits my lungs as he flicks his ashes right into my face.

"Fucking *Lost Boys* wannabe!" I slam my fist into his back.

Someone passes by. A woman wearing a sweater and boots stares, but when she looks up at Prey...

"Little sisters. You know how they are. Am I right, Karen?" I can hear the cocky smirk in his tone.

Her face flushes bright red and she scurries off.

"Fucking cock-corpse! Put me down!"

7

"I would, but then you'd stop with all the pretty compliments, and my ego could really use a boost lately." Another long drag sends another flurry of ashes into my face. "Tell me more about my dead hard cock, Pretty Pet."

My fists clench so hard my nails sink through the skin.

"Where are you taking me?" I huff.

"Home. You've been ordered to stay home for the next seventy-two hours." His cold palm against my thighs burns right through my jeans and sends a shiver slinking through my body. "We could have done this the easy way. You could have just left and let me follow you for the next three days, but no. You had to be a literal pain in my ass."

He jumps over a puddle and my forehead bounces off said ass.

The grinding of my teeth is all I can do. I fold my arms and try to keep warm in my thin long-sleeved shirt.

I didn't dress to be cuddling the dead today. He's dropping my body heat just from being near me.

"Then just put me down and you can walk me home."

"Sounds so much sweeter when you say it like that, Pet."

My fists tighten beneath my arms as I roll my eyes hard.

"Want me to buy you flowers too?"

I keep my eyes closed and just try to endure the torment.

"If you count all of our little meetings, we would be well past the third date, you know? I hear that means something for you prudish human bitches."

I exhale slowly.

Only two blocks. Two blocks and I'll be home.

"Tell me, do you prefer cotton... or lace?" His big palm slides up my thigh and he pushes hard over the curve of my ass. "I bet you're a cotton cunt, huh?"

And that's the last thing he says to me before I decide I've had enough.

My palm bites into the back of his neck, holding his head firmly while my leg rises up as high as I can manage.

Then my knee clocks into his nose so hard I hear the crunch of bone as I'm falling. The sidewalk comes up fast and my palms break my fall with biting pain scraping into the skin. I'm on my feet and running before he lets out his first curse word.

Or even his second.

The sounds of my sneakers scuffing pavement and the slamming of my heartbeat become one and the same. It's a psychotic symphony of sound filling my ears that just urges me to run faster. To make it back over to Crimson Road. I have to get there. I have to get over the line.

I have to see my sister.

I turn the corner sharply. It's an alleyway just before Crimson Road. A rusted dumpster gives way to the rotting stench of old Chinese food. It's just up ahead. All I have to do is make it just around that dumpster.

It's just a few feet now...

It's right there!

It's—

Something solid strikes the back of my skull, but the pain doesn't sink in as warmth slides down my head and hair. I blink, and then hands lock around my hips as I fall.

But never land. Black spots caress the edges of the sky as I stare up at the white and gray clouds.

And then Prey's sneering smile gazes down on me.

"It was just a question. Fuck! I have nothing against cotton panties, Vega." He kneels down between my thighs. I blink slowly at him and try to remember why I came this way to begin with. He shakes his head slowly, his smile faltering as he looks away. "Everything's a mess. And now you are too."

His arm slips beneath me and I curl into his chest as the whole world slips away from me.

"Why did you have to be twins?" It's the last thing I hear him say. It's a strange statement all on its own but the sadness in his tone is strangest of all.

TWO

Kira

There's a knocking in my skull. It's the pound of pain that throbs through my head like thoughts trying to claw their way out.

I wince as I open my eyes to the dark, moonlit room. *My room.*

The floor creaks when I slowly sit up on my beige bedroom rug. A shiver races through me from how damn cold it is down here. The sheer green curtains on the wall to my left hint at a full moon above the sparse night clouds.

"What time is it?" I ask myself in an agonizing groan.

"Almost one o'clock in the a.m," a rumbling voice answers.

I fling my head up so fast the room spins with violent colors.

"Prey," I hiss at the man lounging lazily on my bed. His ankles are crossed and all I can dwell on are his dirty boots on my mother's quilt.

"Whyyyy was I tossed on the floor while you're making yourself comfy on my goddamn bed?"

His lip curls back as his fingers spread across his chest in feigned insult. "Pet, have some manners. I'm a guest."

"You're an assailant. You're lucky I don't report you."

"Mmmm and who might you report me to? The human police?" His laughter cuts through the dark. His perfect white teeth shine in the shadows, so much so that the points on either side are emphasized like the animal that he is. "You're all weak. Even your protectors."

That's the thing about vampires: They think they're so far above everyone else. They think they can take and use and kill whoever they like. They think the little rules and regulations from their council balance and justify their nasty behavior.

It doesn't even come fucking close.

Just ask my sister.

"Where—where is my sister?"

I don't want to fight with him anymore. I just want to know that Kyra's okay.

His smile slips away, fast.

Are they ever genuine for him? Does he even feel happiness? Amusement? Anything?

He drags his dusty boot up my green blanket and rests his arm on the bend of his knee. He doesn't look at me. He studies the moon instead.

He can't look at me.

"Tell me she's fine. *Tell me!*" I'm shaking, and it's no longer from the chill in the room.

"Stop talking," he says in the rasp of a breath. Barely a whisper.

"Just fucking tell me!"

In the skip of a heartbeat he's in my face. His inky hair fans into place as he breathes down against my lips. His eyes darken, their pale blue is stained with emotion and blood in his gaze. Long fingers snatch a hold of my jaw and he makes sure my eyes are locked on to the violence contained within his.

"I. Said. Stop. Talking."

His teeth are bared to me, his fangs flashing out. His breath beats down on my tongue as I stare up at the man who I once thought was my sister's boyfriend.

And he won't tell me that she's fine. She's okay.

She's alive...

"She's dead." I blink up at him, unable to fully close my mouth as I try to bring air into my lungs with shaking breaths.

His hold on my face loosens. The bright red color in his gaze seeps out and the bitter blue comes right back. A lost look lingers there. It reflects my own sense of misplacement.

"She's dead... *again*." My voice shatters on those words.

My heart hurts, but for some reason the pain isn't as breaking as it was the first time around.

Or maybe it is.

"Stop... stop crying," he whispers.

I blink, and wetness clings to my lashes as silent tears streak down my face. Tears I wasn't even aware of until now.

And then his hand slides down my neck, across my shoulder, down my arm. His cool touch rests along the back of my hand. But he doesn't hold me. He doesn't embrace me in his arms and try to smother my sadness with his affection.

He lets me feel every cutting emotion.

It's not at all like it was the first time she died.

"Why couldn't she just stay dead!?" I scream the words out. They're a secret thought I've whispered a thousand times in my own head.

"Why? Why couldn't she leave me blissfully unaware of.... YOU!?" I shove the vampire's hand away and he lets me go without a struggle. "Fucking vampires! Why? Why couldn't you just leave her dead? Why... why did you give me her grief... *twice?*" I stutter out the last word as I slam my fist into his chest.

His subtle exhale is the only indication I hit him at all.

I hit him again against the solid build of his unnatural body, and he lets me. He just takes it. Again. And again. And again.

Until the sobs stuck in my throat creep out and I fall forward from the pressure it releases in my heart. I slump forward, and he doesn't react. My tears bleed into his shirt. The light feel of his fingers along my back are hesitant at first, but then his palms smooth down my spine and he holds me like he's the only thing that's keeping me from collapsing from the force of too much anger and sadness... and guilt.

He picks me up for the second time in one day, but this time he's sweeping me off my feet and cradling me against him. Flawless steps, barely moving my body at all bring us to my bed and he places me in the middle. He curls up behind me, his arms still wrapped around me in an intimate way that calms my heart.

But that's not what I want from him.

I don't want him here.

He hates my kind.

How dare he try to twist his hatred into something it'll never be.

"*Get out.*" I say it so quietly it barely leaves my lips, but I know he hears me.

He releases me slowly. Space suddenly feels colder against my back as he moves further away on the bed.

"Get out of my room."

He pushes off from the mattress and doesn't make a sound as he stands. I still feel him there, staring at me from the edge of the bed. A second slips by. Then I faintly hear the click of the door as he closes it behind him. It's the only indication he's gone. I blink through the tears I can't seem to stop, but I refuse to make a sound. I won't show my weakness to one of them.

I won't.

Because my sister was indestructible.

And look what they fucking did to her.

―――――――

When pale sunlight creeps across my bed, I lie there in the warmth of it for hours. It crawls over the room while I hide beneath the blankets and think about all the things I've already dwelled on through the long dark hours of the night.

I tried to protect her. I was her only friend.

And I failed her.

Twice.

I swallow that thought down. It's a weird sense of grieving I'm trapped in. Because my sister, she truly did die two years ago. The woman I've met and maintained a relationship with during the time since, she wasn't the same girl I grew up with. She wasn't the twin who understood my every thought.

She was... frigid and proper. Scared almost.

I know why.

Of course I understood.

But it's hard to mourn someone you've already lost a long time ago.

The emotions within me are a pushing and pulling confliction of ups and downs. She's gone, but her heart is at some form of peace now.

Finally.

When I shove out from the blankets and sneak into the bathroom, the cold flooring sends chills across my flesh. I leave the light off as I brush my teeth at a slow and distracted pace.

Wow, you'd think I was avoiding a monster lurking in my living room.

Probably because I fucking am.

I know Prey is still here. *Seventy-two hours,* at least. I wouldn't be surprised if he continued to check up on me for the rest of my short mortal life. That's what the council of Crimson City does, they keep tabs on the suspicious.

And I'm sus as hell in this case.

Do they know I checked up on them last month? I surveyed the house. The House, I suppose I should say.

I spotted the man Kyra described, the cruel one everyone fears.

I just wasn't fast enough to kill him before he killed her...

With a swipe of a wet rag over the dried blood along my temple, I realize I've stalled as long as I can. I can't ignore the bloodsucking leech in my apartment any longer.

I slip through my bedroom and quietly open the door.

Then I fling my fist out so fast that the man looming over me doesn't even have time to react. My knuckles meet the hard plane of his abdomen and he folds on impact. The lazy lean he had as he lounged against the door frame crumbles in half a second. My tired eyes watch while Prey hisses out a lost breath as I simply walk past him to my couch and curl up there with my morning blanket. Once I'm wrapped like a pretty cocoon, not yet ready to spread my wings and fly, I acknowledge the coughing creature.

"Put a fucking shirt on and don't get comfortable in my house."

He slowly lifts back to his impressive height, but there's a new glare in his eyes.

"Did your sister never tell you not to attack your superiors?"

Superiors.

He can call himself whatever he likes, but he'll always be the kind of monster humans whisper about.

I hold his crisp blue gaze without blinking. "So your kind can attack us, but not the other way around?"

His hand still lingers on the etched lines of his lean stomach and the smile he gives me is on the cutting edge of hostility.

"Vampires are consensual beings."

"Bullshit."

Prey stalks toward me like the predator he really is. His long fingers brace against the back of the couch as he cages me in to hold my gaze.

He smells like a surprising mixture of honey and spice. I stop myself from leaning in closer to the addicting scent.

He isn't hot coffee. There's no lustful humming or orgasmic eye flutters when I smell him.

Shit, did I just hum?

"To be fed from is the most erotic sense of pleasure you could ever know, Pretty Pet," he whispers. "There are more than enough volunteers. We do not need to attack."

My foot extends fast and hard, slamming into his stomach once more. A groan rumbles from his throat as the air heaves from his lungs in one big huff.

But he manages to catch my ankle. And he holds me there.

"You don't need to attack. But you still fucking do!" I accuse through clenched teeth.

With a flash of fangs, his own sharp teeth shine back at me. "Do not. *Ever*. Attack me." His nails bite into the skin just above my foot.

I refuse to wince from the pain.

Blood slides down my flesh from around his fingertips.

He's controlled. He won't bite my leg off simply from

catching the smell of blood. But the ruby color shadowing his pale blue eyes is a telling sign.

"*Let go,*" I grind out.

His glare burns into mine. Beneath the soft throw blanket my fingers dig into my palm and every calculated way I can think of to hurt him circles my mind.

How to make it look like an accident?

A slip of the pencil to the eye: death by guy liner. A thousand flat-iron burns: an e-boy's tragic demise. Introducing him to Andy Biersack: A fanboy's heart failure.

I don't have time for any of those scenarios, unfortunately.

Instead, I leap off the couch and tackle his ass to the floor with a heavy thump. Prey releases a grunt of pain, but that pain is given right back to me as we flip suddenly. He shoves me down before the air hits my lungs again. And then his hands are around my upper arms, holding my hands above my head as he stares down on me with more spite than I've ever seen from the conniving vampire before.

He hates me...

Our breaths clash between us and there's no gentleness as we glare at one another.

There is nothing but animalistic violence in the air.

Until...

"You were told to protect her, not fuck her," someone says with laughter kissing their warm, deep words.

From my low-lying spot on the floor, I look over the small coffee table to find two—very large—men standing there.

With luggage.

As if they're planning to stay a while.

Motherfucker!

THREE

Kira

The first man strides in as if this has been his apartment for years and he's happily reunited with all his beloved possessions after a long time away. Probably has renter's insurance or some shit. His luggage —an old Bull's duffle bag— gets tossed on the couch without care. He kicks his enormous sneakers off haphazardly near the door, flinging dirt over the beige carpet as he goes.

The second man sets his duffle down quietly and I appreciate him as he slowly slips out of his shoes and closes the door behind him. At least one of these assholes has manners.

Then his hand grips the bottom of his green shirt and he pulls it up slowly. Inch by glorious inch of smooth bronze skin reveals the deep lines of his abdomen.

My eyebrows lift high, but that's the only outrage I'm capable of expressing. My brain is detesting it, complaining about the audacity, but my uterus is already bundling up a little egg and preparing it like a present just for him, whenever he's ready.

He folds the shirt, but when he unbuttons and drops his jeans, my brain finally clocks back into work.

"Who the fuck are you two?" I sputter from the floor, still trapped and held prisoner in my own house by the jerk leaning above me.

The man is folding his jeans now as well, his innocent and smiling eyes finally meet mine, as if he forgot I was here at all.

Yeah. Y'all invited me to your housewarming party here, asshole. Please acknowledge me!

He kneels down on his hunches, squatting in nothing but a pair of tight black boxers and a bulge that not even Mother Mary could ignore.

He sweeps his long golden blonde hair from his eyes, giving me a gleaming smile like the sun rising over a crashing ocean.

"Vuitton," he extends his big hand an inch away from mine... the one that's held down to the floor where I've been pinned.

I pause, but awkwardly lift my wrist as much as I can. He proceeds to shake it like the weird gentleman that he is before releasing it.

My hand drops to the floor like a dead fish, yet still he lingers.

"Louis and I are guards."

"Wolves," Louis corrects.

"Wolves," Prey rolls his eyes hard.

"Don't be mad, little leech. It's not our fault that our senses are so superior." Vuitton is still smiling that big aloof smile he walked in with.

"Louis and Vuitton." I blink at that.

Vuitton smiles, like a dog about to pounce a tennis ball.

"Your sister named us. We're her personal guards when she needs us."

"*Were.* We *were* her guards," Louis corrects once more as he pulls his shirt off and gazes intently out the foggy glass window that overlooks my quiet street.

Guard dogs.

My sister had a pair of guard dogs.

And she named them after shoes...

I blink up at the enormous beautiful man as I try to sort out the mess my life has become.

Kyra Vega had a vampire assistant and two pet were-wolves for protection.

And still her enemies managed to kill her.

"How did she die?" I ask so quietly, but the room halts on a dime the moment I say those words.

Prey finally loosens the pressure he's been holding over my wrists. He releases me slowly, and it's with a hard frown etching his smooth features that he leaves me lying there. He stalks off toward the kitchen without looking back at me.

Vuitton looks to Louis, but the two of them remain silent.

I close my eyes and just wish I could fall right through the cracks in the floor. To be absorbed into the carpet and floor-boards and hope that that existence feels better than this crushing grief. As I lie here wishing for numbness through the anxiety and confusion, Vuitton finally speaks in a gentle rumble of words.

"Someone did it while she slept." His honesty lights up the darkness. His soft words reveal what Kyra already knew would happen.

Exactly what she warned me about last month.

Someone would hurt her there.

Again.

"They found her lying in her coffin just before sunset two nights ago. Other than the four of us and Royale, no one else knows." The enormous man is still lingering at my side. I stare up at him, dissecting those last words.

"Why does no one know of her death? Why isn't it being investigated?" I fling myself up then and look at Louis for more information, but the man hasn't shifted his eyes from the glass window even once.

"Why do you think we're here, Pretty Pet?" Prey says in that cruel and cutting tone of his.

He leans against my kitchen wall as he gazes at me like I'm a toy to be played with.

I process his question, and only one answer comes to mind.

"I'm a ploy. A trap for whoever did this to Kyra."

Edged laughter rumbles from the vampire as he throws his head back and really enjoys what he seems to see as stupidity.

"You're her twin. The twin no one knew about." He tilts his head at me. "No one knows Kyra is dead."

My memories flicker through all the twin swaps Kyra and I did to mom. Our friends. Our teachers. Everyone. They all flash before my eyes over and over again.

"You want me to be bait... in your world."

Vuitton doesn't meet my searching eyes, but Prey just smiles at me. He smiles in that way that makes me think he might eat me alive if everyone turned their heads away for longer than a second. My stomach drops just imagining being planted among the deadliest creatures our world has come to know. And I'm supposed to trick them long enough to catch a killer? The numbness I had craved so badly finally settles in.

"Royale will be here after nightfall. He's too old to sun-walk like I do. He'll get everything in order for you," Prey shoves off from his leaning spot and flops down on my green velvet couch.

Still shirtless. Still acting as if this is their home and not mine.

"Hey!" A banging resounds through the room. "Hey, that's not your stoop. That's not yours!" More ruckus than I've yet heard from Louis erupts as he bangs his forehead off the glass not once but twice, scolding someone down below the entire time. "Tie your dirty fucking shoes somewhere else, bitch! This ain't your building. Keep walking. Yeah, you better keep going, you loose-laced cunt."

My wide eyes blink slowly attempting to process all of that.

His every muscle is taut and flexed as he continues to chew the woman out from the safety of my second story apartment living room. The fog his breath leaves against the glass is smudged from how he's rubbed his chin and nose on the window too many times. Vuitton looks wildly interested, his brown eyes big and watchful as he hops up and strides over to his friend.

"She won't be coming back here any time soon," Vuitton encourages, clapping Louis on the shoulder as the two nearly naked men appraise their good work.

And I'm left sitting on the floor. More confused and worried than when I first woke up.

FOUR

Kira

I'm still glaring daggers at the three strangers in my living room as I sip a soda in my kitchenette. Louis and Vuitton still guard the window, barking their asses off anytime someone so much as spits gum on the sidewalk. Prey naps... do vampires nap? Anyway, Prey lounges with his dark lashes fanned over his sharp cheekbones on the couch, his feet hanging off the edge as he rests.

The last few rays of the warm sunlight halo the two shifters in a golden god-like framing of perfection. Louis' dark brown hair sits high at the back of his partially shaved head. The bun is so loose I have no idea how it's made it through all of his many outbursts this evening.

Vuitton and him are in sync. But they don't seem to be brothers. At least their polar opposite appearances wouldn't suggest they're even vaguely related. But they do share something. It's more than comradery, it's a bond of some kind. When one spots something amiss down below, the other immediately picks up on a silent, unseen cue.

I watch their every move from over my drink and that's

how I know what they zero in on this time isn't a jogger running at "too suspicious of a pace", or a stray cat looking "too stray for this neighborhood".

I know it's something real when they both hone in on whatever it is down below.

Neither of them make a noise.

They simply look to one another with that bond of theirs communicating so much more than meets the eye.

What is it?

"Royale's here," Vuitton announces calmly.

Prey snaps up in a blur of movements. In the time it takes me to swallow my drink and lower it to the counter, Prey finds his shirt, smooths it down, slides into his boots and is already swinging open the door before anyone even has the chance to knock.

"Royale," Prey says with a bow of his head. An odd welcoming passes between the arrogant vampire and the man named Royale. Prey never looks up. He doesn't meet the man's pale gray eyes. Prey steps backward for Royale to enter and it's then that I note that Louis and Vuitton also refuse to meet the stranger's sweeping gaze.

Royale appears as intimidating as these deadly men are treating him, if I'm being honest. His height alone is a fearsome stance of total dominance. He strides into my home wearing a tailored blackout suit that hugs the wide span of his chest. His silk ebony tie gleams, even in the dim lighting of the living room. The stubble along his jaw is the only unkempt part of him. If you could call that perfectly etched five o'clock shadow unkempt...

He's a prowling monster.

Who happens to look entirely like a sex god.

His scanning attention falls on me and I'm suddenly all

too aware of myself. Even while I refuse to shift beneath his slicing gaze.

"Kyra…" he whispers suspiciously.

"Kira," I correct, my arms folding across my stained high school jersey as he appraises me.

The man glances to Prey, but the vampire doesn't lift his bowed head.

"Prey was *right*: you *are* identical." His tone caresses syllables here and there and grates against them at other points.

It's an alluring accent that I can't quite pinpoint.

"Except I'm human," I say those words hard and enunciate them for his little critter brain to fully understand.

"Yes…" He nods while a line forms between his eyebrows, as if me being human is really ruining his precious evening. "Prey will take care of that."

My head tilts at the stranger.

"You have three days. I've told Zavia that Kyra is out of the country for the rest of the week. That gives us three days to prepare." Royale strides back toward the door and out into the hall as if that's all settled.

But it's fucking not.

"Excuse me!" I rush after him and only when I pass does Prey lift his head slightly. I storm out barefoot onto the worn floorboards of the building's hallway. "What if I don't want to? I have a great job, you know? I have an enthralling life. Friends. And family."

Kind of.

Sort of.

I mean, maybe my mother's phone call once a week is the only time my phone rings, and maybe Robert's dick pic is the only one I've seen for eight months, but that's irrelevant. This is my life.

And I have a choice.

"You have no choice," Royale echoes absently before turning his back on me and walking away.

"I'm a fucking human!" I screech.

In the blink of an eye he's on me. His hand presses forcefully against my mouth as I'm slammed into the wall.

"Do not," his pretty grey eyes blaze into a darker, more ominous color before he finishes, "make me turn you."

His breath fans over me in a rush of heat that seems to burn my cheeks as his words sink in.

They truly could. They like to preach that they're all about consent, that the euphoria of feeding is enough to convince any human. But my sister is —*was*— walking proof that consent isn't really their style.

I stare at the monster who is pressed against me so hard that I can feel every part of him.

He really could turn me right now, and his life would be all the easier for it.

He owns me now.

The force of his hand lowers slowly, but he keeps his forearm pressed into my chest for so long the squeal of hinges turning revives a real fear within my heart. My attention darts to the door across from mine.

Fuck. My old neighbor, Miss Croot.

The vampire doesn't even look her way but I know, I just know she'll ask and prod and berate me with her endless questions if she's given the chance.

So I don't give her that chance.

I shove against his strength and with the little space I do gain, I lunge into it. I slam my lips to his so hard that my teeth sink into my lips with the taste of copper filling my mouth.

And his.

The groan that leaves him is barely released as he sucks hard against my lower lip, swirling his tongue across my blood, my mouth... and my tongue. He kisses me deeper, it's a wanting caress that edges on violent seduction. My lashes flutter and I fall heart and soul into the calming and all-consuming sensation he provides with just a press of his lips to mine.

It's like floating. Like flying. Like dying. It's like all three rolled into one.

I faintly hear a mumble from an old woman, but I've forgotten her name. I've forgotten my own existence.

A claiming hand pushes through my hair and when it twists through my locks, my entire head flings to one side with an audible crack that might have just killed me.

Maybe it did.

But the pleasure that's surging through my mind and body is still pulsing deeper and deeper. A slickness glides across the side of my throat. Warm breath tingles across my flesh. One inhale. Two. Three...

And then he releases me.

He steps back one foot after the other until far too much space separates me from the intoxicating man I want to give myself entirely to.

"Why'd you stop?" I blink through a haze of confusion as his hooded gaze slices into me.

He assesses me from my toes and leggings, he pauses on the mystery stain at boob level on my jersey and then tops it off with the slight tilt at the bun that's tied messily atop my head. There's a lost look in his gaze.

I don't know what it is. Maybe he's seeing the train wreck in all its glory and is currently second guessing the identical part of 'identical twins'.

"Listen to Prey. Do your fooking job. And maybe, just maybe you won't die." His shining black shoes swivel and he storms away from me. He vanishes with speed in a matter of half a second.

My throat is painfully dry as I swallow and continue to stare into the emptiness of the hall. I lean there for so long a prodding of footsteps steals my thoughts, and there's the oblivious culprit now.

"New boyfriend, Kira? He's a handsome one, that one. And such a fine, fine suit! You know, I've heard of sugar daddies, I'm not completely out of the loop. You could tell me if you needed someone to talk to. I know you so rarely get visitors, I'm a friend if you need me." Miss Croot's big brown eyes look up at me as she holds her mail in her left hand and the pink leash of her old dingy white poodle in the other.

The poodle looks up at me in pity, as if to say she gets this shit all the time.

"He's not my boyfriend," I finally tell her in a lost voice that's too hoarse to really say much else.

"Mmm, so he is a sugar daddy."

"No," I shake my head, but the thoughts inside are still muddled from the vampire's kiss.

A cool hand slips into mine and I'm torn away from my churning mind as Prey pulls me toward him, his free hand slipping around my waist as he leads me back into the safety of my own apartment. He's shirtless again, and his hair is eternally messy. One thing is different though...

"Come back to bed, baby," he says with a bizarre and unfitting smile. A charming smile. A totally misplaced smile on his psychotic fucking lips.

What in the Ann Rice fanfiction is wrong with this vampire? Did someone feed him after midnight?

Prey nuzzles along my throat as he looks over my shoulder. I catch him giving Miss Croot a dramatic wave of his fingers and a wink before he kicks the door shut behind us. The door slams closed with a rattle and a gasp heard from the other side. And that signals the end of Prey's performance. His hand drops from my waist and he turns his back on me.

"Okay. Let's get to work." He claps loudly, causing the two wolves to jump at the sound of it.

I'm still dazed and numb.

But I do know... I'm officially in a life or death situation with four. Addicting. Fucking. Lunatics.

FIVE

Prey

She's weak. How she's even supposed to be blood related to my mistress I'll never know.

She stumbles once more and it's her damn posture that pisses me off the most.

"Straighten your shoulders!" I shove against her slender frame, and she wobbles at the slightest push of my hand against her body.

Weak.

"Why do I have to practice appearances when I still don't know anything about the layout of the world you're wanting to throw me into?" she whines.

"Because if you can't walk in stilettos, Kyra's favorite fucking shoes even, you won't make it one step into the world we want to throw you into. Vampires live forever. They have plenty of time to pick people apart. They'll know in a single second just by your appearance if you're a real or a fake." My jaw grinds hard and I can't help but drag my hand down my face. I'm exhausted. She's exhausting. "Now, straighten your fucking shoulders."

Her glare is a seething thing. At least that matches Kyra's.

That might be the only thing.

"My life comes down to the fate of a pair of shoes?" Her eyes narrow harshly on me.

"Your life comes down to the fate of knowing who Kyra Vega is, inside and out." My jaw grinds so hard it sends pain shooting through my skull.

"She's my twin!" The human girl says exasperatedly.

"*Was*. She was your twin. Before she was a vampire." I close my eyes slowly to the annoying girl I've been left accountable for. "Tell me, what was something she loved before she was changed?"

That hate in her eyes ignites as she shakes her head.

"Life." My heart stutters at the sound of her simple reply. "Art. Writing. She loved everything and everyone, and then... and then you fuckers should have just let her die in peace. Because the woman I met with once a month for the last two years wasn't the free spirit I grew up with. She wasn't the "fun twin" like everyone always told her." Her eyes dampen just slightly, but she blinks that emotion away furiously as her words continue to teeter on a scream. "She was serious and alert, and informed on every single thing that happened in Crimson City. Because that's what happens when you're deathly afraid of the person who raped and turned you into a monster. So yeah, as I fight for my life with you blood sucking zombies, I'll be just like her, I'm sure." She folds her arms in a huff, but still sways a bit in the four-inch black pumps.

I roll my eyes in frustration, despite how the dull beating of my heart sinks for her as well as my mistress.

"You're right." I say on a slow exhale, and she too is surprised by my agreement.

Until I lift my fingers, settle them along her smooth, delicate shoulder and give her a nice shove.

Her ass bounces to the carpet with a firm thud.

And if I thought she was angry before...

"You fucking Bram Stoker fanboy little bitch!"

My brows lift at her insult while Vuitton chuckles himself into a howl from across the room. His laughter distracts me for only half of a heartbeat, but her arms are around my knees in less than that time, and I can't catch myself as she hurtles me to the floor. She climbs my body like I've envisioned Kyra doing so, so many times before. I can't help but react with a repressed groan as her legs straddle my hips, lifting the hem of her evening dress up her beautiful, pale thighs. My dick is still throwing a lone celebration until I see the sunlight glinting off of a sharp metal blade. The large kitchen knife in her palm is a misplaced item that I can't even process her holding.

"Where did you get that?" I continue to ask curiously as she presses the length of it against my throat.

"Where was she hiding it?" Vuitton asks with a bit too much awe in his voice.

My hand lifts and I run my index finger along the sleek metal handle, tracing her knuckles as I go.

Her elbow flings back and the hard end of the Susie Homemaker weapon jabs into my mouth. An ashy taste of blood washes over my tongue and I fucking hate it! Vampire blood isn't pumped and cared for as vigorously as human blood is.

It's the closest thing to feeding on a corpse as there is. That's why it's like slowly dying as we age. Even a sunburn could scar us for life.

But we try not to say too much about that around the humans.

"Do not." I take a deep breath but it's not enough to calm me. "Ever. Strike me." Every muscle in my body tenses as I control the urge to flip her on her back and bury my head in the soft crook of her neck, just to drain her dry. "Let's ah... let's all calm down now," Vuitton says carefully from just behind the mad woman.

I notice neither him nor Louis actually removes the rabid human girl off of me. Real friends, through and through.

Kira's lips curl as she looks down on me for another long second. Then she flings her leg around and she's on her feet, striding away from me in the heels she couldn't even balance in just moments ago. The nice curves of her hips sway along with the dress. Her long blonde hair wafts in the air behind her as she storms off.

She's undeniably sexy now.

Confidence. And Anger. That's the key to fooling people. Nothing could make her fit in more like blazing rage and a fiery ego.

So maybe, just maybe, she could pass as my mistress.

Or maybe she'll get us all killed.

Only time will tell.

SIX

Kira

"Never question yourself. Do not ask if you can or cannot do something. You're a high council member. Number Six, to be exact. You have one superior, and she's honestly never around to check up on if you're Kyra or Kira. So just act like you're above everyone and everything and you'll do fine," Prey explains with a wave of his hand.

"So the other five. What are their names?"

"Five?" He arches a dark eyebrow at me.

"You said I'm number six. If I'm Kyra, it might benefit me to know the names of my coworkers."

"Council members. You don't have coworkers."

My jaw grinds as I sit lazily on the couch with my legs tucked beneath me, trying hard not to show my ass in this obnoxious dress.

"And their names are?"

Prey's eye twitches.

Who the hell assigned this asshole to be my sister's assistant? What does he even assist with? Continuous migraines? Permanent pains to the ass? The urge to dick punch him every eight and a half seconds?

"Croft one, Zavia Laurent. Born in Lille France when the city was just conquered and claimed. She is your leader, your Council Queen, and she will not bother to even look at you. Take comfort in being too far beneath her list of priorities."

There's a notebook on the coffee table, I fling it open and I'm scribbling her facts on a blank page, even as he starts on with the next member.

"Croft two, Pavel." Prey visibly shivers just saying that name, but he doesn't let it delay his spew of information. "Pavel is an elder, and second in command. He—" Apparently this vampire isn't among Prey's favorites. "As vampires age, they..." his head tilts this way and that. "They *do* age. And... it shows."

He seems to shake those morbid thoughts away.

"Croft Three," he continues.

But my line on Pavel is nearly blank. I've learned almost nothing about the man. He's the second in command, and he's elderly. That's it.

"Wait. You didn't even give me a back story on Pavel. What's his last name? His history? Anything would help." I know from work as an independent investigator that the devil is always in the details. Even if I was just tracking cheating husbands instead of deadly vampires.

"His last name." Prey pushes his hand down his face as if he could just wipe away his annoyance.

He clearly can't.

"If Pavel could remember that far back, I'd give you his last name. I'd give you a cute little how he was made backstory. But Pavel is old. He's... literally ancient. And he doesn't remember tedious details like his last name." The vampire sighs a long and drawn-out sound of irritation.

"Croft Three," he says once again and instead of pressing him for more, I move on to the next line. "Rival Royale."

A snort I can't repress shakes through me, but Vuitton is the only one who joins in with my snickering.

Prey simply arches one of his e-boy eyebrows.

"He made that name up, right?" I'm still smiling hard. Prey's just tries glowering harder.

Okay. Noted. Not made up.

"Rival is the advisor and speaker of the council. You will be in contact with him the most. He and I arranged for your role in the absence of Kyra Vega."

I jot that down and note that I'm no longer getting pretty back stories, but just the facts. Prey isn't patient and honestly, facts are always worth more than stories.

Usually.

"Croft four is currently vacant, but will be filled by an appropriate candidate soon."

"Empty?" I ask.

Both Vuitton and Louis peer over their broad shoulders at me, and the stark silence that settles in after my question lays a blanket of eeriness over the room.

"Yes." Prey carries on. "Croft Five—"

"What happened to the vampire in charge of Croft Four? Did they pass away?"

Prey closes his eyes slowly, and his tolerance with my hunger for more information is very obviously wearing thin.

"Croft four was found dead twelve nights ago." Louis says from across the room.

My heart stutters.

"Um. Hold on. Time the fuck out." I stand suddenly and face Prey. "Is this a common thing for vampires? Members of your immortal council just fucking drop dead on the regular?"

Prey's attention shifts over my face, his gaze scanning. For what? I don't know.

He lowers himself lazily into the spot on the small green couch that I just vacated. He kicks his feet up on my little coffee table as he goes.

The asshole.

"There have been some... *issues* recently. Creature Control is investigating, but a small group of us are looking into it ourselves. Hence, recruiting a pain-in-my-ass human to delay everyone from finding out Kyra Vega has been murdered."

My pen itches to write down all those words that stand out in his explanation.

Issues.

Creature control.

Delay...

I try to process each of them slowly.

Issues is his pretty way of saying someone is slaying vampires. Important ones. I already knew their kind were deadly. I just didn't know they killed their own kind. Until Kyra warned me when she last visited me during an unapproved meeting in my own bedroom.

That's how I knew it was serious. She never bothered to come see me aside from our monthly catch-ups. If she risked coming here to see me, I knew she was scared. She spoke of her rape and how she was turned.

I try not to think of it now with Prey watching so closely but the memory of the fear in her eyes creeps in every day.

I can't help it.

The notebook in my lap calls back to me.

What I don't have any details on whatever Creature Control is.

"What's the Creature Control?"

Prey's head leans back and his eyes close as if he's asking God himself why his perfect afterlife is being tormented with my questions. His feet hit the floor and his legs spread wide.

"Creature Control is Crimson City's body of law and order. They're equivalent to the FBI of your world," Vuitton tells me thoroughly. "Louis and I are agents for Creature Control."

Aww. He's such a good boy, of course he's a critter cop.

The way he kneels on his hunches, soaking up the sunlight against his smooth golden skin gives me the immense reminder of how puppy-like he really is.

My heart settles. It's a strange elation when someone calms you without even trying to. Maybe Prey finds me annoying, and the other vampires don't care if I live or die, but at least I'm not completely alone in all of this.

"She's back!" Vuitton bangs his forehead off my newly smudged glass window and Louis perks right up as they both turn irate.

Over what, you might ask?

"Not again," I whisper to myself.

"She ran past this building three times in the last hour!" Vuitton's shoulders flex as he stands tall before the window.

"You're fucking right, she has." Louis slams his hand wide open against the wall and their eyes are so wide they're bulging. "Running by here three times. She's got some balls." The two of them fog up the glass as they huff in unison. "Come down my street one more time you flat-footed floozie! See what happens!"

Their heads swivel as far as the laws of physics will allow them, until the menacing jogger passes out of sight.

Vuitton claps his friend on the back once more, both of them beaming with pleased smiles plastered on their obnoxious faces.

These are their police?

I sigh heavily and turn my attention back down to the vampire dozing on my couch.

"Croft Five, Aston Cardence." He doesn't even look at me, which is good. Because the moment he says that name, my heart thunders to life. I try to keep a straight face. "You won't like him. And he'll make a point to make sure you don't."

I swallow hard.

I wait for him to say the one thing I'm waiting for.

Say it. Say you suspect him!

"Croft Six—"

My breath shakes as I cut him off. "That's it? He's mean, that's all you have for me?"

One of his eyelids creeps open as he makes little effort to look at me. "That's it. He's an idiot, and he isn't important."

I shift on my feet and try to swallow down the apprehension that's crawling through me from everything my sister told me about the cruelest man on the vampiric High Council.

Tell me they've looked into Aston's whereabouts during my sister's death.

"Croft Six—"

"How many deaths have there been in the council this month?" My jaw clenches, despite how hard I inhale and exhale through the grinding of my teeth.

"Why are you so impossible to train? Why can't I just give you the information and you accept it? Council issues are none of your business."

He stands then, and his lean height towers over me. Slitted eyes like a snake's glare down on me.

"I'm putting my life on the line, and for what? Closure? What are we stalling for?"

"To hinder CC investigations." Vuitton fully turns away from his perch at the window now, giving me his full attention. "CC has jurisdiction over all supernatural crimes. Vampires have their own council, wolves have their own pack, and pixies have their own pods, but the CC are neutral outsiders. Rival thinks someone within the vampire's council is responsible for a few human murders and the last two killings that have occurred within the council. He wants to delay Creature Control from stepping into the Council's domain. He doesn't want the lower vampires to start doubting their superiors. He wants the council to handle it internally and quietly. I've agreed to help buy him a little time. He's using you to delay the inevitable."

My anger lowers. How does he manage to do that? How does this mangy shifter ease every tense thought in my mind with just the soothing rumble of his voice?

"Two?" I ask innocently.

Prey doesn't give a shit about my need to know, but Vuitton does.

Vuitton is the sweet one.

"Croft Four died first about a month ago. And your sister, Kyra Vega died two nights ago." Prey folds his arms hard across his chest. He's so wired with strength and protection that it literally seeps out of him.

And into me.

I knew there was another vampire who died before my sister.

Kyra said he was getting reckless. That he was becoming too controlling and daring.

I just didn't do enough to help her before it was too late.

And now my life is on the line too.

SEVEN

Vuitton

Humans sleep so restlessly. I'll never understand what these creatures have to fear when all the monsters are lurking in a different zip code.

Kira turns over once more on the tiny queen mattress. The bed would barely sleep myself, but I suppose it's comfortable enough for her petite size.

Shit she's small. Breakable... bendable even.

The thin sheet shifts around her and the black lace of her panties are revealed along with the smooth curve of her ass. My brow lifts as I watch her from the doorway, toeing the line between protecting and creeping on her all at the same time.

"Wasn't Edward totally creepy for watching Bella Swan?" Louis pipes up in barely a whisper from where he leans, just near the window.

I look away so fast, I regret not memorizing the little moaning sound she makes just before I close the door with a soundless *click*.

"Edward was a creep. And a vampire," I correct.

"Ah, so it's only creepy when vampires lurk over sleeping women?"

I pause to really articulate my response.

"No, it just seems to happen more frequently with vampires. A creepy little hobby for some creepy little undead creatures."

I push my hand through my hair and try not to dwell on the fact that my partner is absolutely right.

I'm being a fucking creep with this woman.

But fuck, someone better be watching over her. Someone needs to help her along.

Instead, it seems like everyone else around her is happy to just toss her into a pit of death and watch her squirm.

Shit.

That got a little too serious.

Kyra always told me to be as calm and happy as I try to make everyone else.

I wish I could be.

It's better if I hold on to my worries and process them over and over again until they consume me. That's what keeps everyone I know safe.

Because just look what happens when I don't. You can see the results of when I distance myself and try to focus on my own health. Just look at the fucking mess of blood I've made! And it's all because I couldn't love the woman who took care of me.

And now I'm obsessing over the shadow of her memory.

The one who's now sleeping restlessly in the next room.

EIGHT

Kira

Days pass with little to no information being offered to me. Dresses and shoes and how to part my hair and hold my shoulders are all it seems Prey wants to focus on.

On the surface, in this tight navy dress that makes my eyes seem more sapphire than gray, I really do look like her. My hair is pulled back so tight it hurts. My spine is so stiff I swear it might break from the strain. But my steps glide like perfection when I strut past the critical vampire for the twelfth time in an hour.

It's only now that I realize, my sister truly was a stranger to me. I can't remember her laughter ringing out like it used to even once over the last two years. She wasn't the life of the party any longer. Her face was so smooth and flawless, smiling lines could never have disrupted her perfection.

I'm standing here, three inches taller and so formally poised that I feel like I might fall apart with even the smallest of stumbles. This is supposed to be who she was? This eternal frowning pull of my lips, this is who they made my sister become?

It's tragic.

"I think you're perfect," Prey praises. It is literally the first positive feedback he's ever given me.

"What was that again?"

I'm clearly not used to any form of kindness from him. His face becomes serious once again as he too realizes the error of his ways. He shifts from one foot to the other.

"You're decent. As close to my Kyra's flawlessness as your lowly human self can perform." He nods slowly, happier with that backhanded compliment.

We're far too uncomfortable now. We have no idea how to function side by side unless we're clawing each other's eyes out while attempting to strangle one another.

This—this basic kindness shit is weird.

"Thanks," I mumble.

He smiles, and this time he truly smiles. It isn't a sneer or a cocky grin. It's... genuinely sweet.

Why is my heart warming? No! I will not accept bare minimum, borderline insults from beautiful men and allow my neurotic heart to think it's flirting.

... Is it though?

I give him another look from the corner of my eye and I note his attention gliding down my frame, along my throat, my breasts, my hips, my long legs...

No! Eye fucking is not flirting, Kira!

... Isn't it though?

"I'll inform Rival," Someone with more brain cells than my infatuated mind says.

I turn and spot Louis making his way to the door. Still shirtless and animalistic, but obviously uncaring of what anyone in the outside world might think of him.

He doesn't say any more before he closes the door and silence settles in with his absence.

What just happened?

"Rival?" I ask.

Prey grabs his shirt from the floor and pulls it over his messy dark hair. "We're all set. We leave tonight for Crimson City."

My heart freefalls.

"T—tonight? You want me to go with you to Crimson City tonight?"

Vuitton's attention perks up and he looks away from his post at the window. He seems to check on me fully just by noting the shaking sound of my voice.

"You should rest," he says with that soul touching rumble in his tone.

"I cant!" I nearly shriek. "I'm not ready! I barely know the names of the council by memory. I have no idea what all of them look like. How am I supposed to address anyone?"

"You shouldn't." Prey shrugs flippantly. "Don't address anyone. Give vague answers. Just do the bare minimum to get by. You do not want to make any friends here. We only need you for a little while. A month at the most."

"A month?" My hand trembles, and I have to fist my fingers into my palm to stop myself from lashing out at him. "A month is not a little while."

"A month is barely a blip of time at all. Someday, when you're old and failing, you'll come to understand that." His cold blue eyes cut into me.

Why is he always like this?

He's charming and cruel all at the same time. Who turned this beautiful man into something so dead inside?

"Come on," Vuitton opens my bedroom door for me and I've never felt so used in all my life.

I pause and look at the two men I'm trusting with my life. And for what?

To find Kyra's killer. To look her rapist and murderer dead in his eyes and take his life from him, just like he did to her.

My pulse speeds up. I keep pacing, I have to keep focused. My goal is so similar to theirs, but I don't want to just investigate.

I want to avenge.

And I will.

An hour seeps away, and still I stare at the flat white ceiling of my bedroom. The sun blazes warm light into my chilly apartment.

I can't sleep.

Instead I go over my facts:

Zavia. Pavel. Rival. Aston.

Zavia. Pavel. Rival. Aston.

Zavia—

The squeal of hinges slices through my anxious mantra and I sit up beneath my thick blanket to find Vuitton lingering within the partially open door.

"May I come in?" He waits tensely and I can't help but see how different the polite shifter is in comparison to the asshole vampire who would have just stormed into my room, stolen my blanket and attacked me with my pillow on his way out.

That's where the myths got it wrong: Vampires clearly don't give a fanged fuck about any formal invitations.

I nod, and the room holds so much quietness as he comes in, closes the door and slowly makes his way toward me.

He's carrying something small in his large hand, and he offers it to me when he's just at the edge of the bed.

I take the little stack of polaroids from his hand, and not

only do the pictures seem tiny, everything around me, including myself, suddenly looks minute in the shadow of his massive stature.

The confusion within me fades when I turn the pictures over to find faces and names scribbled across the bottoms of the white sections.

Rival Royale.

The handsome vampire who threatened me in the hall stares up with a brooding look of seriousness. His lips form a hard line across his hard features. The lighting of the flash seems to have smoothed his appearance into a vision of impossible perfection.

But there is one remarkable thing that strikes me.

"So, vampires do show up in photographs." I smile to myself and wonder what else the legends and stories about these monsters got wrong. "Where did you get these?"

Vuitton shrugs his shoulders like it was no big deal. "I stole them from the Council's filing cabinet."

I smile even harder.

As does he.

"You got them for me?" I look up at him from beneath my lashes as he nods slowly. "Thank you."

I slip Rival's picture to the back and find a beautiful redhead featured in the next picture. Her green eyes are so piercing and knowing, I realize who she is before I even read her name at the bottom:

Zavia Laurent.

I slide her to the back as well and the most strikingly man appears in the next photo. The angles of his cheeks and the sharp lines of his jaw are as deadly beautiful as his pure white smile. Bright pink hair rises into a messy mohawk atop his head. Fangs come down to a point that brush against his full lower lip.

Aston Cardence.

My stomach twists hard.

He's the cruelest man of them all. He's the one my sister told me was a nightmare come to life. He's the one who turned her, then raped her, and I'm certain he's the one who killed her.

I close my eyes slowly, memorizing his face more than any of the others.

I shake away the thoughts and flip his picture to the back.

A woman with a big smile and long black hair as dark as her eyes is in the next one.

Acessa Milane.

My brow lowers as I look at the pretty young woman.

"I thought there were only six crofts." I remark as I trace the edge of the thick film.

"Seven. She's the newest. Her space is just to the right of yours." Vuitton explains.

"Who's to the left?"

"Aston."

My lips curl, but I do my best to hide my disgust.

I can't believe my sister had slept next to her tormentor day in and day out without murdering him herself.

I shake my head as I look at the final picture.

The moment I slip Acessa's picture away, my hands tremble as the next man—no, monster—stares up at me.

A pair of eyes so hollow they're depthless black holes beneath heavy pale wrinkles that hang loosely from his fore-head is the most dominating trait. His hair is nothing more than a few white strands draping down from his bald head spotted with age. His teeth are rotting black, and two rotten fangs protrude out from his dry lips.

Pavel.

He's the nearest thing to a walking corpse as I've ever seen.

And suddenly what Prey said about vampires aging makes so much more sense. He's ancient. He truly is.

I stiffly place the pictures face down on my nightstand and try to breathe out the uneasy feelings tangling tightly in my stomach.

I'm walking into a nightmare.

I should rest. I know they'll all be up until the dawn, and I'll be expected to do the same. But I'm too anxious and wired to sleep.

"You should practice some meditation or breathing exercises. Your heart is a bit faster than theirs, but right now it's a slamming noise that is much too loud to belong to a vampire."

I peek open an eye at the shifter.

"How do their hearts beat?"

In movies, their pulse is nonexistent. So how can I blend in if even Vuitton can hear every beat of my anxious heart?

"They still have a pulse, but it's just different from a human's or even my own. Mine always sounds like yours does right now. Shifter hearts speed nonstop, while vampire hearts maintain a slow rhythm. The nearest thing to death as I've ever heard. It's just enough to keep them living, but more than enough to keep them from dying."

I exhale the slowest sigh, and though I can't immediately tell if my pulse is calming, Vuitton nods with a sweet smile at my attempt.

"You can do this," he whispers like his encouragement is a secret he doesn't want Prey or Louis to know about.

"Thanks." I roll my head from side to side and try my best to release all the tension I've been carrying in my shoulders since these men stormed into my life.

"Come here," he steps closer and I hesitate for only a

moment before I sit up and lean into the one person who has been a friend to be during all of this madness.

Do I trust him? Ab-so-fucking-lutely not.

But he isn't an enemy. I can tell that much at least. My sister took him in because she trusted him to protect her. That speaks to his character some.

I just don't know if I'll ever be able to trust anyone in the supernatural world.

His big hands lift cautiously and I have to force myself not to shift beneath his touch as he wraps his warm palms around my shoulders, just under my neck.

And then he starts kneading.

I hold his gaze as he delicately works the stiffness from my muscles. His pace is slow and firm and it all feels oh so fucking good. A shaking breath slips from my lungs when his thumbs press just right and the smile that pulls at his lips is wide and alluring.

Charming.

Perfect.

The touch of his fingers is hypnotic. Their very presence is an addicting sensation, like the rush of adrenaline just before a fall.

My defenses subside and my shoulders slump while he works my body like he knows every inch of it. I unknowingly lean in so far that my temple brushes against his smooth skin. I tilt my head up to find myself just a kiss away from the hard lines of his abs. Lines carved as if from granite cut through his solid muscle tone. A heavier breath pushes from my lungs causing him to shift as my exhale washes down the thin trail of hair that leads down the lowest part of his stomach. Down. Down. Down...

My gaze lowers, and then lifts back up.

His light brown eyes pulse with a deep green ring around

them. His hands against my body halt entirely. All that exists between us is the way he looks at me right now. It's a hot spark of energy, a fire of want.

A blaze of lust.

His head dips forward and I don't even think about it as I sit up on my knees. His hands shift. My chest presses against his, but it's still not enough.

"Vuitton?" I ask in the breath of a voice. Barely a sound, not even a word at all.

More of a moan.

Then he presses his lips hard to mine, parting my lips and tasting the desire lacing his name on my tongue. The warmth of his hands shift, and the strength of those palms slides down my body in a controlling and delicious way. I arch into him as he wraps his hands around my thighs and slides my body up against the bed. He positions me just how he needs, his thickness is hard between my thighs, his hips nestle perfectly between mine.

Then I realize he isn't using my body for himself at all.

He positions himself just a fraction of an inch over me. His hold on my thighs slips around my hips, and then his fingers are teasing along my stomach, just over the button of my jeans. Warmth flashes across my flesh in a shiver that shakes all throughout me.

His kisses slow down. He pulls back just slightly, allowing our gazes to shift over one another. Our breaths clash in the air between us.

As he second guesses his actions and my desires, I make it totally clear for him.

I just want to drown in the energy he gives off.

Perhaps it's the human part of me firing off warning flares, or maybe it really is some kind of supernatural magic.

But I want more of that addicting spark that's glowing between us.

My fingers slide from between his, just to unsnap my jeans before I slam my lips back into his. A groan shivers between our mouths and I'm honestly not sure if it's mine or his. The flick of his tongue against mine spirals unending energy right through my core, but it's nothing compared to the static sensation that blazes over my flesh the moment his warm fingers trail down my abdomen. It's a casual pace, an exploration of my soft skin against the roughness of his palm. It slows even more when his fingertips dip down, then sneak beneath my jeans.

My back arches to help him get to where I want him to go faster, but he simply maintains that leisurely pace of his touch. The heat of his fingers stop just above my clit, so I'm forced to grind myself against his palm.

This time, the low rumble of pleasure is *definitely* his. It's a delicious sound that sends a whimper from my own lips as I thrust my hips once more against the frustrating space between his hand and my wetness.

At the sound of my want, he kisses me harder, so hard it hurts, but fuck it also feels so good.

And then...

Cold sweeps in as air flurries my hair and before I can even open my eyes, the crack of wood is sounding through the room as his hand collides with the nearly open door. It jars shut with a harsh slam against his palm.

Vuitton's eyes are a wild timber color. His blonde hair is a mess across his bronze features and there's even aggression in his posture.

As for me, I'm still panting like a mad woman who just fucked the memory of a ghost. And that ghost is long gone now. I'm alone and spread wide on the tangle of my blankets.

The span of the bedroom separates me from him as we stare wide eyed at one another.

I can't believe we just did that.

I just fucked this stranger's hand, and now he's all but running for the door.

"I—" An apology of some bizarre sort is on the tip of my tongue, but it gets cut off.

"Knock, Prey!" Vuitton growls, his hand curling into a violent fist as he continues to hold the door shut.

"It'd be my pleasure." A taunting tone says from the other room. "But it sounded like... *trouble* in there."

The word trouble spins through my head. I sit up slowly and Vuitton still watches me like I'm the most dangerous creature he's never come across in all his life.

His free hand that was against my sex just seconds ago lifts, and he holds my gaze for a second longer. His fingertips slide over his lips and he tastes me with hooded eyes lowering down my body, his dark gaze now tinged with remorse and something more.

My thighs shift involuntarily.

A long drawn out exhale falls from his lips. So much is unsaid in the way he looks at me one more time. And then he turns his back on me, slipping out the door without another word.

He leaves me there with nothing but the pounding of my heart to keep me company.

That... and an incredible sense of frustration.

NINE

Prey

He slinks out of the room quietly, like a beaten dog who was never given a bone in his mangy life.

Good.

The fucking horny barking mutt.

"You were going to fuck her!" I accuse on a furious whisper.

"I was *not* going to fuck her," he growls back while he folds his arms across his chest.

He's doing it to make himself look bigger. It's a typical defense pose that every animal in nature does when they're threatened.

Newsflash asshole: you're already as big as a goddamn dumpster fire. With the brains to match.

No matter how much you puff your chest out, you'll still outweigh me by a hundred pounds. And I'll still kill you regardless.

I tilt my head at the dog. I shame him with just a stare. I'm *this close* to rubbing his nose in her pussy and reminding him that we don't shit where we eat.

My thoughts get sidetracked by that visual for only a moment.

"Don't fuck up again," I say as I poke my index finger into his puffed-out chest. "Wouldn't want to get her killed the way you did with Kyra."

My lips tilt up into a cutting smile that twists up the emotions that are already eating my heart alive.

His jaw grinds. The warm brown at the center of his eyes chases out the ring of green in his iris. His beast wants to come out so fucking bad to test me.

Test me, motherfucker! You'd be one less memory of my mistress I'd have to live with.

TEN

Kira

I stand at the window of my bedroom. My pale hair is pulled tightly back, my brow feeling entirely too alert because of it. The crushed red velvet dress is perfectly form fitting, it stops just above my knees. I don't sway in the four-inch red bottom heels as I watch the deep orange of the sunset bleed over the buildings along the horizon.

I only have minutes left in this reality I've known all my life.

The moment darkness falls, my whole life will bleed away into it. I'll be *her*. I'll be a High Council vampire, and all I'll have to protect me is the surface appearance of what that power looks like.

Honestly, the surface appearance is all I really knew of Kyra in her afterlife. She gave me glimpses here and there of what happened to her, but never anything about who she really was.

Prey is right, my relationship with my sister was stale and fake. It was a bond we both wanted to keep, but we didn't know how.

She wanted familiarity.

I wanted closure.

Neither of us got what we wanted.

My head leans into the cold glass window. It feels good to let it soak into my pounding head that's reeling with the mix of too much and too little information. My palm settles there too, with the comfort of the cool glass against my sweaty palm.

A cracking noise snaps across the glass. The cold stings against my skin and I pull away with a pained gasp.

Only to look up at the man directly outside.

Outside my second story apartment.

His short dark hair blows in the breeze. The suit jacket slashes back and forth against the single button holding it together against his black dress shirt. The silk ebony tie flurries sideways violently, but he just stares at me with the same stern look he left me with in the hall after the strangest kiss of my entire life.

"Kyra," he mouths, but I can't hear his voice as he speaks quietly near the glass, frosting it over with ice simply from his breath.

His hands lower and his biceps flex against the smooth material of his suit before he flings the window open. The lock snaps at the top and the metal of it clatters to the floor. Then he's crawling inside. He's prowling, and I'm backing away from the wild look in his eyes. He's storming, matching my every step and I'm slipping away from him on careful heels that are just begging to be kicked off and abandoned.

"Rival," I say formally.

Politely?

How am I supposed to address a high vampire?

Sir? Mister? Dark Lord of the Night?

He closes the gap with one dominating step, and then his hand is threading through my tightly tied back hair with a grip of pain right at the root. He slams me against the wall, releasing a gasp of anger and confusion from within me. Then his mouth is against mine in a claiming kiss that steals my breath away.

As well as any rational senses I might have owned.

My fingers grip his smooth tie as my lips part. I press into him as much as he presses into me, because something inside me is crawling up and grabbing onto the allure that he carries. It's some kind of energy. It's vertigo. It's a vibration that syncs into me with all that he has, and I want that unsteady delicious feeling to live inside my heart for the rest of my fucking life.

"Kyra," he groans against my mouth.

And just like that, the vibration strikes to an abrupt halt.

My fingers release his fine silk tie, one diligent finger at a time. My palm settles there and I shove him off me as I try to find a breath of fresh air between us. He staggers back, but not because of my force. He's... dazed it seems.

The man who threatened my life less than seventy-two hours ago now looks torn between caressing my face and breaking it in the palm of his hand if I get too close to him.

Clarity begins to shine through in his steely eyes. He assesses me in a new light, from the top of my high ponytail to the points of my sleek black heels.

"I suppose I passed your test," I arch a perfectly manicured eyebrow at the infuriating vampire. "Mister Royale?"

He swallows hard at the cutting sound of my tone. Dark Lord of the Night would have had the same effect, I'm sure.

His hands move swiftly as he adjusts the windsor knot of his tie, his stature shifting back into the deadly confident man I first met.

"I suppose that you'll have to do," he finally replies dryly.

My lips curl into a sneer.

Asshole.

"Grab your purse. Nothing else," he instructs.

He doesn't even look at me as he strides to the door and leaves me behind.

Emotionless. Rival Royale is an emotionless creature. Or, at least he pretends to be.

I ignore his hostility and turn to the small rack of dresses, heels and clutches that Prey set up for me in the corner.

He really is a fantastic assistant. No wonder my sister kept him around for as long as she did. That has to be the reason, because it sure as shit couldn't have anything to do with his sparkling fucking personality.

I grab the largest handbag, though it's still no longer than my forearm and no thicker than a Bible, but I'll have to make the most of it.

I abandon my driver's license, I don't even think about my debit or credit cards, and I don't search for my apartment key.

I don't need any of those things anymore.

The one thing I'll need in my future is that kitchen knife.

I pull the blade from beneath my pillow and the moon-light glints off of the edge of it. Sure it's no dagger, but Gordon Ramsay would be super impressed, I'm sure.

And it's all I have at the moment, so it'll have to do.

I slip it into the black clutch. My head lifts high, shoulders back, ready to walk right into their world.

And by the end of it all, I'll slay that motherfucker who hurt my twin.

The three men walk casually with me down the apartment stairwell. I pass Miss Croot and her wide eyes ping pong between the entourage of the gorgeous men who flock me as well as my new, crisp business woman attire.

"Goodnight, Croot."

"Ww—g'nightt..." she stutters while Prey winks at her and strides on by like the delinquent prep boy that he is.

The moment Vuitton swings open the front door, the stinging fall wind bites into my barely clothed body.

"*Fuck!*" I hiss and pull back from the sidewalk. I scurry back toward the building, but Rival jerks me right back out.

He holds his hand around my shoulder like I'm nothing more than a leaning post for him.

"Prey," he says with a firm nod my way.

Prey bows his head oddly and before I can utter a single insult, the vampire sweeps me up with one palm beneath my thighs and the other curled intimately around my back.

"This is not Twilight! Put me down, you glitterless Edward Cullen fuck!"

"Glitterless?"

"The glitter was the best damn part. You're a dim comparison!" My jaw grinds against itself in protest, but my teeth still try to chatter from the cold.

A slow smirk pulls at his lips and it's almost strange to see. It shines in his eyes with thin little lines meeting at the corners of his cold gaze. It's genuine amusement from the heartless vampire.

At least I think it is...

It could just as well be allergies.

Constipation?

A seizure?

I may never actually know.

In the next several blurry seconds, the city lights of Chicago streak like a stream of fire overhead. It's a hellish sight of falling stars through the night sky that is both beautiful and terrifying all at once. Thrashing wind claws at my hair and captures the air in my lungs. It's such a breath-consuming, dizzying experience that I have to close my eyes and shield my face into Prey's soft black tee-shirt. His fingers digging into my thighs ease and his thumb brushes oddly back and forth there. I focus on that sweeping sensation against my skin. Once, twice, Three times—

And then we stop.

My lashes flutter and I pull my head up from his cotton shirt to find him staring down at me. There's tension in his brow. A concerned sort of appearance that I'm just not comfortable receiving from someone so hot and hostile one minute, and cool and calm the next.

I'm all too aware of his body, and of mine. My fingers that are clinging to his neck lift, and I don't know why I just slightly brush them over the bottom of his messy hair.

My heart seizes.

I have to be deadly careful of my heartbeat from here on out!

And I will be.

"Put me down," I finally whisper.

I don't look at him. It surprises me how gentle he is when he lowers me down his hard body and lets my heels click against the sidewalk before finally dragging his hands away. One hand grazes the open back part of my dress and a shiver races after his touch as he skims his fingers down my spine.

What the fuck is happening?

Why is my pulse sounding alarms right now?

I inhale slowly and exhale even slower.

Everything will be fine.

I count the drumming within my chest until it's no longer something I can hear, but only something I'll depend on dearly for the next four weeks.

Stay alive.

That's the only goal when you're a human walking into a den of thirsty vampires.

If I'm not careful, I could end up dead... or worse.

Something looming sends a spider crawling chill across my flesh. My attention drifts to the moon haloing the lone building just past the draping vines of the willow trees surrounding us. Through the dry leaves, the spikes of the church can be seen piercing the starless sky. The jagged metal sheathing the tips of the pointed roof top are as ornate as they are ominous.

But there's not a single cross in sight.

But it's still a place of religion. It was once a house of God, though now its faith is one of a different kind.

A very, *very* different kind.

I think back to when I snuck up to the property of Hell after Kyra's confession that she feared someone within the council. Some vampires can walk relatively freely in the daylight, but they're still very much creatures of the night. I had spied on the cruelest vampire: Aston. He was exactly as my sister described: Heartless to the core.

I spotted him cornering Kyra. I knew who he was by her body language during their simple interaction: from the way she repelled away from him, but he just kept going. He kept on antagonizing her. It was quiet in the bright afternoon hours as I watched through the window. And I was just as quiet while I plotted his gruesome death.

I'll finally be able to make good on that plan.

Today I'll walk in as Kyra, and walk out as a killer.

And knowing that no one will ever have to fear the man who took so much from Kyra ever again, that will be enough to ease my conscience.

I'm skipping too far ahead, though. I can't think about that right now. I have to focus on... not breaking my very mortal neck in these monstrously high heels. It's pathetic that this entire plan of theirs could crumple all because of a sprained ankle.

I lift my head high, straighten my shoulders to an impossible standard, and stride down the smooth brick sidewalk.

I only make it a few steps before I get pulled back into the brushing limbs of the tree. They sway around my hair in the cold breeze. I peer up at the dark eyes searching my face.

Vuitton's worry isn't a mask like Prey's. The line between his eyebrows is deep and his apprehension in his gaze goes even deeper.

"Be careful, Kira," he whispers as he steps away. "I'll be watching. Keeping you safe."

That's sweet. He sounds a little creepy, but the situation calls for some borderline stalking, I think...

His palm slides down my arm and around my wrist, toying with my fingers before he lets go. And then he turns away.

His enormous body grows in size. It's an impossible sight to witness beneath the white light of the moon. His shoulders widen, his neck thickens, and his entire frame morphs and grows into a beast of a man. As he runs off into the night, the sound of cloth tearing accompanies him. He carries on with a howl of animalistic excitement and human pain tinging his melodious cry to the moon.

My wide eyes watch him until the night completely absorbs him into the darkness.

"Where is he going?" I ask, trying to reclaim my lost breath.

I thought he'd accompany me the entire time. I thought I'd have his help. I thought I could depend on one fucking person at least.

"Wolves, especially members of Creature Control, do not enter our domain without an invitation." Rival doesn't seem concerned in the least, and the sound of his footfalls are a command that forces me to turn away from the shifter.

And makes me accept that ultimately, I'm in this alone.

Just as I have been for the past two years.

Prey walks just a step behind me, and I'll admit he's good at playing the part of the dutiful servant.

For once.

I pretend not to be aware of him at all as I follow Rival up the many stairs to the front of the enormous, towering cathedral. I don't gawk at the decorative metal that lines the heavy door, or the way that dark metal can be found lining every seam of the foyer. It's like a crown molding straight out of the dark ages.

My heels clicking rhythmically over the stone tile flooring is the only sound that can be heard. The ancient building emits a gloomy atmosphere that seems to settle right in and makes itself at home under my skin. Thick gray curtains made of fine silk hang from the high ceilings and cascade down to a fraction of an inch above the smooth stone floor. Though the walls are painted black, a carved mural of a crucifixion still lines the wall directly in front of us, just above a set of opened double doors. It's like a mouth leading into the stomach of the church, and I have a pretty good idea about what lies in the bowels.

When we cross the threshold of the doors, Rival's palm burns down the opening of my dress and his touch across my skin nearly makes me stumble. There's a clatter of heels and a gasp of air as I teeter uncertainly.

Then, just before I fall, he's pushing me against the wall, staggering my steps even more in a loud clattering of noise. Cold stone scrapes my spine as his warm hands cover the small of my back before the softest lips press desperately over mine.

And just like that, my messy fall is turned into a messy, confusing, conflicting, all-consuming kiss.

The petite and polite sound of someone clearing their throat drags Rival away from me. My thoughts blot back into my lust-filled mind once more, and I have to try hard to appear like I'm not sedated by his simple allure.

"You may have missed her, but you don't have to be rude, Royale," a woman says with a soft laugh warming her words.

She's an enchanting vision of perfection. Ruby red lips are full against her bright white teeth with two sharp points pressing down along her bottom lip. Her dark brown eyes are somehow glimmering in the glowing yellow lighting. The emerald dress she wears flares daintily around her smooth thighs.

There isn't a single flaw to be seen on her slender frame.

Not one... aside from a faint splatter of blood against her chin.

I smooth my dress and try to think of what my sister would do in this situation. No, not my sister. The sister I knew would have laughed loudly and charmed this vampire den like it was a frat party.

So what would a spy do? What would I do?

My chin lifts higher, and I slip past Rival with our chests brushing lightly, my palm smoothing down his sleek black tie as I go.

"Acessa," I say her name in greeting like it's honey flowing over my tongue. I try not to look her in the eye as I pass, not out of fear, but I give my best to just breeze through the room like it's been my home for the last two years and not just the last two minutes.

Two men lean against the wall, both of whom are missing

shirts, and one of whom doesn't seem to be aware that his pants are unzipped all the way down. Both are in a daze, staring forward with hooded eyes that seem to see absolutely nothing.

I ignore both of them as well while I casually step over their legs to make my way to the table.

Without question, I take the chilled red wine from the long dining room table. It's hard to keep my pulse calm as I pour a meager amount into a crystal glass.

I can't focus on anything. Everything feels much too important, and yet I have to seem aloof to it all. My hands settle on the table and I push up to slide myself on the edge, crossing my legs as I sit carelessly before the three of them.

Rival arches a dark eyebrow at my perch. Acessa keeps her beautiful smile in place. Prey catches my eye, and there's a slight gleam there. His smirk is a cutting thing, and it feels testing but prideful all at once.

"How was Milan?" The woman asks with her big curious eyes.

I buy myself some time to think by taking a sip of wine.

My tongue curls back from the liquid the very second it touches my lips. The thickness of it alone is enough to turn my stomach.

Because it's not wine.

It's cold blood.

Oh my God, is it their blood? My eyes dart to the two shirtless men. So many thoughts race through my mind: *Spit it out! No! Swallow that shit! Swa-llow. It!*

I have to sit here and freeze this fucking charming smile in place as the chilled blood soaks into my tongue like battery acid on a sponge.

Until I'm finally able to swallow it down.

My throat constricts. My lips curl within the plaster of a

smile I hold in place, and it nearly comes out my fucking nose as I hold in my cough.

Never once does my smile fall.

Acessa waits patiently and enthusiastically for my reply the entire goddamn time.

"Beautiful. As. Aa-always," I grunt out, trying hard for effortless poise, but sounding more like an alley cat with a bad coke problem instead.

The snorting sound of Prey's laughter shakes through the room, but Acessa and I continue to smile pleasantly at one another.

"Ah, I wish I could go. I do wish I can leave our home soon." She keeps chatting while I flash my attention to Rival, who just looks as impassive as ever.

Why don't all the vampires leave this place?

"How was Markin and the European den?" Acessa asks.

Ah... yes. Markin. And the other Euros... Um. Well...

Fuck.

"He was the same old Markin," I give a little insider-joking-laugh at the end of that vague little remark and thank the ever-loving fuck that Acessa laughs along with me.

Prey snorts annoyingly once more, and I want nothing more than to break his nose so he never gets to make that arrogant sound again.

Why the hell did no one brief me on absolutely anything besides shoes, posture and handbags?

"Do you want to rest, Darling?" Rival asks so intimately I nearly blush.

I can't do that. Nope. I can not allow blood flow to rush anywhere, north or south. None. Can't do it.

I dip my head low and sweep my sweating palm across my cheeks in an attempt to steal away the warmth in my face.

Fluidly, I slip down from the table and stride toward the man who is apparently so devoted to my sister.

It feels like a violation of some girl code for me to be snuggling into his side as he takes my hand and leads me deeper into the bowels of the church.

"Rest well," Acessa says kindly from across the room.

I bow my head to her with a smile as I leave.

Prey walks slowly behind Rival and I, giving us plenty of respectful space.

He's so good at being bad, and yet so perfect at being a vampire's assistant.

How is that possible?

"Take her to the croft." Rival drops my hand the moment we're out of sight and turns to Prey. "I have to find Pavel. He's been asking about Kyra." Rival strides away down a dark corridor to our right, and I'm left in the shadows with my least favorite Ann Rice character.

Prey nods his head to the side in a 'follow me' sort of way but once we cross the hall that leads to the cellar, I already know my way around from the back entrance here. I've never been to the croft itself, but the windows in the cellar do provide a fairly nice viewpoint for spying.

Prey offers me his hand when we reach the narrow stairs that lead down to a hard drop, and my attention looks from his hand to his eyes and then back again.

"Habit," he whispers like an apology before dropping his offer and slamming his shoulder into mine as he strides quickly down the steep steps.

What exactly was Kyra's relationship with these assholes? How could she stand so much undead testosterone in one house?

Really though, what were their relationships?

Prey seems dead set on making this life of Kyra's as

comfortable and easy as possible. He has had moments of tenderness toward me, but it seems more familiar than sexual. Vuitton... Well, Vuitton has been more than sweet. He's been —the memory of his body pressed against mine flashes through my mind.—

Was he like that with Kyra?

I roll my eyes at myself for letting that stinging emotion flood through my chest.

I quickly file it away to calm my aching heartbeat.

And Rival? Yeah, they were definitely hooking up.

What about Louis, then? The socially quiet but loudly protective shifter comes to mind. Though he was my sister's protector, I don't think there was anything deeper between them.

How many boyfriends did Kyra have in this life?

And if none of them were able to save her from her fate, what does that say about my prospects?

When I take a deep but uneasy breath, I find that we've entered the bowels. And seven crofts are in a line at the center of the room. Each one has a number etched deeply into the coffin shaped tombs.

"You're six," Prey tells me with a sweep of his hand. We walk toward it on slower steps, and just as I stand over my literal grave, someone else speaks.

"I didn't expect you back," the gravelly tone says, "so soon."

The densely packed shadows of the dark room are all I can see, until the corner lamp splashes golden light over his black and white sneakers.

Aston Cardence.

"How have you been, Six?" He asks with a cruel smile that carves dimples into his taunting features.

My heart hammers as I stare at the man who tormented

my sister for the last two years of her life before killing her. *Again*.

"Mistress," Prey whispers with a bow of his head.

The sudden formality he shows me serves as a reminder of my own existence.

Of my pulse, and of what I have to hide.

"Why, did you miss me, Cardence?" I ask on a snap that I wish could lash out physically at his pretty pink hair.

His brows lift high and his pale green eyes flicker with something, but I'm not sure what it might be.

"Oh, dearly," he says with a smirk.

His steps are languid, but with each one my heart begs to push me into fight or flight mode. Yet still I just stare, unimpressed at the daunting vampire.

My heart storms, despite how hard I try to calm myself.

With a fixated gaze he comes closer.

He comes so close his hand lifts and that's all the space that he allows between us. His shining attention flits across my features in an animalistic way. There's a question in his sea glass colored eyes.

Something... bad.

"You look different," he whispers curiously.

Fuck.

My pulse now feels like a mallet slamming into a spike, over and over again.

"Yes. And it's unfortunate that you still look the same, Cardence."

His mouth falls open with a half smirk of stunned shock. "Damnnn, Six," he whispers with growing amusement.

I turn away from him with a flick of my hair and my hands want to tremble badly, but I hold them delicately in front of me instead.

"Prey," I beckon as I stride to croft six.

I wait with blank boredom painted on my face, and I refuse to exhale the painful breath I'm holding within the tightness of my chest. Prey works quickly to push aside my coffin lid for me, and it's morbid that I'd rather crawl into my tomb and die than continue to look at that all-knowing man a single second longer.

Prey places my little handbag in the bottom portion of the coffin before he offers me a hand. I slide my sweaty palm into his cold one and I instantly feel a little better. I feel a gentle squeeze there, and I know the two of them are watching me closely as I climb in. It feels like a trap to crawl into your own coffin. It feels like a lifetime of fearing death is washing into me with the intent of drowning me in a puddle of my own creation.

I slide in.

Smooth, cold stone kisses my flesh.

It's hard to swallow as I accept my fate.

Then I lie down in my tomb, waiting for Prey to close the lid on my existence.

The light squeal of hinges sounds like an alarm as the lid is lowered over my body inch by inch. I watch the light fade away with wide eyes.

Panic slams against my chest. I lie immobile.

A dim crack of light is all that is left.

"Good night, Six," Cardence whispers like a snake slithering in just before all the light is shut out.

And then I'm left all alone.

The darkness feels pressing. My fingers slide back and forth, touching my thighs before slipping the few inches to feel the smooth grain of the side of the sarcophagus. I do it again. I trace the space once more. Three inches. It can't be more than three inches of space on either side of my body.

The shaking exhale I release blows right back into my

face. It's hot and stifling and gives the illusion that there's not enough air in here.

There's not enough air.

There's not!

My palm collides with the top and I push so hard it flings open with a resounding slam. I'm sitting up so fast I nearly leap right out of the damn thing.

But Prey is right there. His hands are against my shoulders in an instant, cool along my damp skin as he stares down at me hard.

"I—I can't stay in here. I—I need to get out!" The look I give him is too fragile, too scared, and I fucking hate it. I was doing so good at concealing that human side of me.

Until now.

"You," his voice drops to a whisper and I realize Acessa is now watching us from across the room with a sparkle in her big brown eyes, "you need to lie down, mistress." He lifts his brows rather sternly.

He's politely saying one thing while threatening me with a lift of his eyebrows.

My jaw clenches down hard and fast. I nearly bite my tongue all the way through.

She's watching. But the man who poses a real danger here is gone.

I'm as safe as I can possibly be for the moment.

I can't go back into that tomb, though.

"No." His eyes widen as I say it, and I widen mine right back at him. "You lie in here and tell me how great it is," I snap at him in a hushed tone that still carries all through the tomb.

"I'd fucking love to," Prey hisses with impatience. And then his hands on me are against the edge of the coffin and he's stepping right into the meager little marble box.

"Stop it!" I push at his legs, but his fucking insulting stability never wavers. He's sitting at my side in less than a second. "Get out!" I say louder.

He simply sighs at me and with a heavy hand against my chest he shoves me down into the terrible dooming darkness that is my deathbed.

"Stop it!" I push and claw at him, but then it happens.

He pulls the lid closed over us once more.

And that pressing darkness falls over me once more.

"Prey! Get me the fuck out of here. Move! Get out! *Now!*"

His arm against my chest never budges. He's curled up against my side, and I can feel him watching me as I squirm.

I'm the prey now.

I'm the living embodiment of the weakness I swore I'd never show these damn people.

"*Shhh,*" he whispers warmly against my neck.

"I—I can't fucking breathe in here. I'm suffocating! I can't do this."

The weight of his bicep across my body shifts, his hand lifts and just when I think he's about to slap his hand over my mouth and force me to shut up, his fingers gently graze my jaw. It's the faintest caress of his cool touch along my flesh. And it drifts, his hand wanders lower as he strokes along my chin and then... he skims his fingertips along my parted lips.

"I can help you," he says it so quietly and ominously that it sounds like the devil himself is making me an offer in the dead of night.

"Help?" I ask against his fingertips.

He lingers there before tracing the shape of my mouth ever so lightly. The warmth of his breath trickles along the curve of my neck and he suddenly feels impossibly closer.

"I can make you sleep. I could give you the most peaceful sleep of your entire life."

"That—that sounds a little too much like death, and I don't think I'm ready for that kind of foreplay in our relationship yet. Thanks, but no thanks."

A breath of a laugh slips from his lips and dances along my neck in such a way that it shivers right through me.

"No. Not death, but the very next best thing. You'll sleep, and then you'll wake up fully rested. You'll be the same. I promise, Pretty Pet." His taunting tone makes me want to kick him in the balls.

If only we had the space.

I hate him, I really do. But… I need him in this moment. I need to keep my cover, and I can't do that if I'm having the kind of mid life anxiety crises that even Kanye would be envious of.

I just don't know how to separate the line of hate and need in my head.

I can't.

"Just do it." I close my eyes hard and try to find what little air that might be left in this fucking death trap.

His fingers slip lower. The feel of his cool touch drifting down the line of my neck is heightened by the blinding dark. He trails lower and lower and lower, until he's skimming along my collarbone in a distracting little taste of what I know he's capable of.

I believe him. I know he can provide me with what he offered.

I just hope I don't lose myself in this deal I'm making with the devil.

"Open your eyes, Pretty Human," he whispers so softly it sounds like a sweet, sadistic sentiment. "I want to see that moment where all that despising disgust in your gaze fades out and lustful euphoria replaces it. I want to see your sensuous hate for me."

My lashes open fast and I try to find him in the darkness, but it's totally impossible.

"What—" I try to ask what's thick on my tongue, but the question dissolves the moment his lips press to my throat.

My mouth opens with shock and that outraged emotion only grows stronger. His traitorous tongue slides along my skin between the open-mouthed kisses he presses swiftly and slowly down the side of my neck.

"What the fuck, Prey!" My palms flatten against his shoulders but, it's only the briefest moment of violent intent.

The curve of his lips tilt up with a cruel smile, and that's the last thing I remember before his sharp teeth scrape against my flesh.

And then pierce my skin.

My muscles slacken. The hard, repulsed curl of my lips fades as a gasp of wanton need sneaks out.

That's what fucked me into this screwed up situation to begin with.

Need.

The anger in me is so far gone now that it might never come back. My palms against his soft shirt are no longer shoving, but clutching. My fingers tangle right into that black cotton tee-shirt like all I want is to pull him closer.

And so I do.

I pull until his body is flush against the side of mine and the demanding need within me settles low in my body. Lower than my stomach. Low in my sex. It pulses there, and I think my blood is pulsing itself along my throat, but I'm not nearly aware of that at all.

"*Prey!*" I gasp as my hand slides lower. I don't stop until my fingertips slide beneath the cotton cloth and start trailing the hard lines of his abdomen.

A groan of his own hums against my throat, and that

initial pain of his teeth is no longer there as he kisses me tenderly. Sweetly.

Lovingly.

"Sleep, Pretty Human. Sleep." His hot mouth drifts higher and he presses a tender kiss to the line of my jaw. I turn to him like I'm drawn to the soothing sound of his delicious voice.

I'm leaning into the small space that separates us. I feel the heaviness of his breath along my parted lips. Every single thing I feel is Prey.

"*Prey,*" I whisper in a trembling gasp.

His hand along my face is light and caressing.

"Sleep, Pretty Pet. Before I change my mind and make you my favorite snack for the rest of your short, miserable existence." There's an audible sadness in his voice.

It hurts to hear. My hand slides along his ribs and I'm simply holding to comfort him now.

As is he. He lets me hold him, and I let him do the same for me.

The beautiful way he feels wrapped around me is all I can think about.

And that's something I hope I'll remember when I wake.

If I wake.

ELEVEN

Prey

    Fuck.

TWELVE

ASTON

His back is to me, but he's greatly aware of my presence the moment the door quietly clicks closed behind me. I know he hears every single detail from the slow stride of my shoes to the warm glass of blood I pour myself in his favorite little study. The bottle dribbles at the end, and a few droplets land on the shelf next to a set of law books.

The small room consists of an entire wall of old musty books, actually. Most of them are so ancient that the bindings are fraying apart. Other than his books, he has a lone leather chair and a messy desk with too many unread notes that he can't bother to waste his time with.

That's Royale in a nutshell though. Boring and wasteful.

Just as he is with Kyra.

I pull a first edition copy of—whatever is nearest, really—and the moment I open it, a thin page crinkles out and wafts down slowly to land in front of my sneaker. I toss the book back down with a dusty slam. It now sits carelessly out of place, and I know it'll drive him crazy.

Whenever he bothers to look my way that is.

The way Royale ignores me is more deliberate today than most days.

Sure he usually hates me and avoids my presence, but today he's displaying a very special hate indeed. And it makes me wild with desire to take it further.

"Good evening!" I say loudly, my smile stretching even more with the idea of making him crack that smooth facade of calm he always carries so well.

Fuck his calm.

I want to see his chaos.

Any little emotion. Any of it. Christ, why is he so chronically boring?

Still his back is to me as he simply looks out at the dark grassy expanse that rolls across the estate. Sure, he can try to ignore me.

But I know I'll win eventually.

I take a long sip of the fresh blood Acessa herself collected this morning. The taste of the new stock washes over my tongue and though he is a stoically boring vampire, Royale does appreciate the finest stock.

"Are you going to tell anyone?" I ask casually as I circle his tiny study. I stumble against the fine rug and leave the corner overturned as I go. I drag my hand along the sleek black fireplace and leave a nice smear of blood across his mantle as I go. The embers inside are dwindling, but still warm.

Just like she felt when I stood close enough to taste the worry in her every heavy exhale.

His lack of a response as he stands like a fucking second rate Batman overlooking Gotham baits me to push him further. Harder.

I need to fucking *break* him.

"Did you grow tired of her?" I take a long drink and drain the cup. The glass doesn't shatter as I toss it onto the stack of scattered papers lining his desk. Blood rains across the pages in a splatter of pretty art. "Did you—did you kill her, Royale?" His knuckles crack as he flexes his fingers slowly into his palm. "She once told me she would have done it to you if given the opportunity." The profile of his face is all I can see, and the strain of his jaw is like cocaine hitting my system after the last three decades of numbness in this goddamn monstrous body. "She said that right before I fucked her, Royale. Right before I made her cum."

It's a lie, but it's a damn good one though. Because it's the one thing that always seems to shake and rattle his cage.

And this time is no different.

Then his hands are fisting into my shirt. He drags me so hard and fast that I can't help the laughter that stumbles from my lips as he slams me into the shelves. Books tumble and break apart as they hit the tile floor with a series of fluttering thuds.

"Shut the fook up, Cardence!" Royale seethes through sharp, clenched teeth. "You don't know what you're fooking talking about!"

My heart nearly patters with fright. I wish it fucking would. I with the quiet thing would hammer like it used to. I wish he'd just lose control.

Attack!

Kill me already!

I smile at the reckless fear in his eyes.

He knows that I know.

Even if I don't really know anything.

"Who's the girl sleeping in croft six?"

"Kyra Vega."

My head slams into his and he flinches hard as our skulls knock, but neither of us feel the pleasant pain like we once did.

But that was a long, long time ago.

It isn't as satisfying as it should be.

Nothing really is anymore.

"Kyra Vega never said a fucking word to me. No matter how much I messed with her. She wouldn't give me the goddamn time of day. So then who is the smart-mouthed woman in croft six?"

He hauls me up in a flash of power and slams me back down into his precious books. They tumble and fall around me like the pages of a history I've seen far too much of. He leans in close enough to... to kill me, really.

And yet still he doesn't.

"Stay away from her. And stay the fook away from me."

He releases me with too much force and just the right amount of anger to sedate my need for emotion. His rage is a soothing balm within my mind.

It's delicious. It's nirvana.

And now... it's gone.

Fuck.

And I'm still left wondering about Six.

THIRTEEN

Kira

Warmth clings to my skin and I wake with a muddle of confusion circling in my mind. A charge like electric energy flows from my toes all the way up through my stomach and comes to rest like a hum within my heart.

"Prey?" I whisper into the darkness.

He's still here.

Watching me, I know it. I can feel it.

"Y-yes," he stutters oddly.

His uncertain tone isn't even remotely hostile, and that confuses me.

What a weird little man.

"I feel... different."

I remember his teeth sinking in. The orgasmic feel of his power still caresses my skin like a shadowy memory.

"Y-yeah," he says on an unsteady exhale.

What the fuck is wrong with him?

His palm skims over my stomach and he holds me. My instinct is to shove him off me, but... it feels like the most natural reassuring thing in the world to have him close.

It feels *good*.

"Will I have a mark where you bit me? Do I need to cover it for a while?"

I think back to the things I left behind in my apartment. Concealer is in my old life. And these flawless fuckers probably can't even fathom needing an under eye cream or even a smidge of makeup coverage.

"Hopefully fucking not."

Ah, there's that asshole tone I've grown used to hearing.

"Okay," I whisper, turning my head this way and that, but not feeling any stiffness where his fangs pierced my skin.

Maybe vampires have a quick healing saliva or some magical shit. Maybe Prey just spits on me a little and no one will know an assistant spent the night feeding on a high council vampire.

"Can any of them read minds?" I ask, suddenly nervous. But seeing as we're both locked up in this tomb, it feels like now is as good a time as any to vent all of my curious questions.

"No," he says with a heavy sigh.

God, why is he suddenly acting like he has a lot of shit to do today?

He is an assistant. He probably *does* have a lot of shit to do.

That's too bad for him. I need answers.

"Why is it that I'm on the council, but you're just an assistant? What makes someone worthy of the High Council of vampires?"

This draws another annoyed sigh out of Prey.

"Power. Once you're turned, your powers, strengths and abilities can vary greatly. You —I mean Kyra— was a *very* powerful vampire. She was just as strong as Rival, that's why they got along so well."

"And they were... mates?"

"What? No! Fuck no. If they were, he probably would have cared enough about her to protect her more."

Ouch. Hostility is truly his forte.

Another angry breath heaves from his lungs, but he continues.

"Kyra and Rival were friends. He let people believe it was more because he knew people didn't screw with her if he claimed her. But she wanted friends. She would never admit it to the others, but she wanted to feel like she once did when she was alive. She wanted some sense of normalcy in this undead world. And Rival saw that in her. He befriended her when she only had me." A heavy pause drifts in between us before he speaks like a ghost of a word. "But neither of us were there for her when she needed us the most."

My heart drops, and I hate that I can relate to the blood-thirsty monster so much right now.

I should have been there for Kyra. There were so many times I wasn't there for my twin the way she was for me.

"What about Cardence?" I think about how he taunted me, and how I saw him act terribly with Kyra once before. He saw right through me. "Were the two of them ever more?"

Prey's scoff fans across my skin and I find myself suddenly brushing my fingers along the back of his knuckles.

I blink at that and pull my hand away stiffly.

"Everyone hates Cardence. He's fucking depressing. He's unique, and a cocky prick because of it. He's an energy vampire. Kyra hated him just as much as we all do."

Then how did he know?

I shake my head.

"Who's the most powerful vampire on the High Council?"

I turn toward Prey in the little space and though I can't

see him, I know his mouth is *so* close to mine. My suddenly stuttering heart is all too aware of him since he fed on me.

I hate that.

"Zavia for sure. She has unimaginable abilities. Vanishing is a true benefit for her. Rival only grew into that power within the last few years." *Vanishing?* "Most vampires grow stronger with age, or through the bond of a mate. Some seek out many mates, but Zavia's powers are her own. She has never taken a mate, and she won't in the future. She wouldn't share her strength with another."

"Did... did Kyra have a mate?"

This question draws another seething breath out of Prey.

"What the fuck is your problem? I need information. I need more than just an uncomfortable pair of heels and nice hairdo to deceive these bloodthirsty mosquitoes for you!"

His hand jerks away from me and light floods over us as he shoves the lid away and storms out of the deathbed I had gotten far too comfortable in.

My jaw clenches hard, but I manage to rise from my sarcophagus. And when I say rise, I don't mean that I'm drawn up like an eerie creature of the night. I have to throw my leg over the edge and literally hurt my coochie trying to crawl out of this fucking stone box.

My heels stumble and threaten to break my neck on the way out.

"Fucking, vampiric bullshit!" I hiss.

But when I stand, Prey is looking at me with wide eyes and an open mouth with no cruel words falling from his lips.

And that's how I know something bad has happened.

"Your neck," he whispers.

"Shit, did it leave a mark? I told you it would. Dammit!"

In a flash, he's so close that I can feel his energy prickling over my skin. And then he's caressing my jaw. Right before he flips my chin harshly to the side and really inspects my throat.

"*Fuck!*" he hisses.

"What? Just get some concealer. You're my assistant, fuck-boy. Run on out to Walgreens and get me a pale shade of concealer. We'll be fine."

"No. You," he shoves his fingers through his inky hair and pulls hard. My hands lift to instinctively make him lower his fists down from his pretty locks.

"Stop," I whisper. "It's just a hickey. It's not a big deal."

Why? Why do I care if he hurts himself?

"No! It's not just a fucking hickey, Kira! Jesus Christ, why are you humans so incredibly dense!?"

My heart dips at the sound of my real name on his lips.

Especially spoken in such a thick layer of anger.

"It's a mark!" He looks up at me with wild blue eyes, like a storm crashing through the calm night sky. "It's a mating mark, Kira," he whispers like he's been slain and he's taking his last breath to give to me.

And it's then that I see the problem.

I haven't just been marked. I've been claimed.

By Prey.

Fuck me.

FOURTEEN

Kira

I want to kill him and hold him all at the same time for doing it. My rational mind argues that he has no control over these things, but my irrational mind is already digging a grave to bury him alive.

"I'm so sorry," Prey says lamely.

He's sorry?

He's fucking *sorry!?*

He hates me! And fate foolishly made us mates? Partners for all eternity!?

My mouth opens but nothing comes out, and I don't even know what I could say to this asshole who is supposed to be out looking for my sister's murderer. Not claiming mates and building white picket fences to grow old with.

"I have to go," I turn away from him on the heels of my shoes and I hear him slowly follow behind me. *"Don't."* That one word stops him oddly in his tracks, and I don't know why he listens, but I'm thankful that he does for once.

I just... everything is just too much right now. Why? Why would the universe make me his mate? I don't want to be in the same room with him, much less love his arrogant, petty heart.

Fuck!

I storm up a set of stairs on the opposite side from where we entered the croft.

I haven't studied the church much, aside from peering through some stained glass windows, and I need to clear my head. Everyone will be resting soon. And while they rest, I'll be doing what I came here for.

Finding my sister's killer.

The staircase here is more ornate than the other cripplingly thin set of stairs. They must be a newer renovation. They twist upward while a pretty metal rail with grooves etched into it guides me toward the upper levels. It's lit by glowing red lights that shine across the tips of my pointed shoes with every step I take.

A large hall opens up at the top. To the right is a small sort of library that spans across an upper level. Books line the walls on all sides. It's a room decorated with rows and stacks of literature. It's painted in shades of biography and fiction, with accents of collected poems. My heart dips and leaps and dips again, all at the same time. I know Kyra would have loved it as much as I do.

The enormous room is quiet and empty, save for a forgotten glass that rests on the mantel above a large burning fire. The embers crackle and I'm tempted to step into the room and stay a while, but my feet keep moving.

Unsure of what I'm supposed to be looking for, I simply map the building out and take mental notes of the layout as I go.

The following room is a large bathroom, and I would pass it by as well, but a glowing display of red lipsticks catches my eye. Various shades and luxury brands of all kinds line each side of the large mirror. The lights above the sink flash on the moment I step in front of it. And then I look up at what I know I'll see.

My long blonde hair is still tied swiftly back, minus a few strands that came loose during the nap in my death bed. My eyes and features seem brighter beneath the blinding white lights of the vanity.

As does the small red marking that has appeared just an inch below my ear. A heart.

It's literally a fucking heart.

Intricate lines slide through the middle of the shape, and they drip down in different lengths and columns in a modernly artistic way.

It's... goddamn it, it's cute.

Fucking *adorable* even!

I hate it.

I close my eyes slowly and wonder what it truly means to be a vampire's mate. Prey said mates can share powers, but I don't feel particularly powerful.

There's a tingling like the numbing sensation of static through my arms and down my fingertips.

"*Fuck!*" I hiss as I try to shake off the weird feeling crawling up my shoulders.

I fling open the black cabinet on the wall and my hands clatter against the bottles of perfume and makeup kept in there. When I find what I'm looking for, I slam the cabinet closed and start shaking out the contents of the pale bottle.

The thick liquid slips over my fingertips and I pat it fervently over the offensive spot on my neck.

Full coverage in a house of flawless immortal vampires. I suppose some insecurities really do follow us all the way to the grave.

The thin red lines of the mating mark begin to hide away

like a blemish that I wish would fade over time. But I know better.

I just don't have time to dwell on giving my eternal heart and soul to some glitterless fuckboy.

I step away from the reminder of what lies beneath a thin layer of makeup and start to explore further down the hall. The deep red carpet is soft beneath my shoes and I sink just slightly as I walk. I stumble, the annoying point of my shoe kicking into the back of the other, and I barely right myself on the frame of a door.

It cracks open. Inside, an old man has his back to me.

Single strands of white hair hang from his head, his skin there sags in the shape of his skull, protruding in great ridges of detail.

The hair on my arms lifts with a shudder shaking my frame.

"Nicco! Nicco, fetch my glasses," the man croaks.

He turns, and his features are a wash of pale coloring and deep purple bruising across his face. His eyes are so sunken in, I couldn't guess the color if I were gazing into them up close. Long bony fingers curl out over a page he lifts to the lamplight on his ornate wooden desk.

I recognize Pavel by the unsettling memory of his photo.

Apparently it's true: eternal life does *not* equal eternal beauty.

Footsteps sound slowly and another elderly man, but not quite a crypt-keeper like Pavel hobbles over to the front of the desk. I pull back just slightly to hide behind the door as Pavel puts on a large metal pair of glasses.

"She's supposed to return today," Pavel mutters, and my pulse nearly stops dead as I realize he's talking about me.

"Yes, master. Ms. Vega and Mr. Royale arrived earlier this

evening." Nicco adjusts his own little black glasses, and the two men stare at one another for a long moment.

"Good. She keeps Royale's head on straight when she's home. Now, where's my blood? Get me my drink before I retire for the day."

I slip away from the two elderly vampires and nearly collide right into a third.

"Ah, Six," Aston's smirk crawls over his face as he looks down on me like I'm his dinner.

"Cardence," I arch an eyebrow at the man I should have just killed already.

"Come again?" he says it so quietly it sends a shiver through my body.

"What?" I narrow my eyes on him.

"Say. It. Again."

My jaw grinds.

"Say what again?"

His smile lifts even more, until two dimples kiss his cheeks.

"My name. Say my name again, Six."

A red hot blush flashes over my face and I immediately turn to look away.

But I can't appear weak.

It's bad enough that I'm appearing less than supernaturally flawless in front of this creep.

Why are all the men in this church such sin-filled assholes? You would think the whole building would spontaneously combust from the sheer blasphemy.

I exhale slowly and pretend to crack my neck this way and that before looking back at the still sneering vampire.

"Listen, Cardence, you don't scare me." The thought of him raping and turning my sister flashes before my eyes and I crack my neck once more to stop myself from lashing out right here and now at a man who could easily rip me limb from limb if he wanted. "You're nothing more than a narcissistic coward who gets off on tormenting women."

His eyes flicker with a hint of red bleeding into the dark embers of green. His fingers clutch into my arms and he rushes me so fast I see stars when my head bangs against the wall.

"And you're an overly emotional wet dream, Six." He's breathing so hard that I can taste his excitement with every word he says. "But you're not Kyra Vega. So... that begs the question: who are you?"

His head tilts curiously as he gazes down on me with manic excitement.

My heart is pounding so hard I swear I might die of a panic attack before he ever gets the chance to put me out of my misery. He's different from the others. He doesn't look like he wants to eat me alive. He looks like he wants to smother me. He's... desperately clingy.

"What are you?"

"*Who* are you?"

I roll my eyes at him and it just makes him smile harder.

Could this weird, pestering, pink-haired punk really have raped and turned my sister?

"I'll answer your questions. Because you're a stranger here, and I just *know* you're filled to the brim with questions. So let me be your guide! And in return, you'll tell me who you are and what you want." He arches a dark eyebrow at me expectantly.

I shift in his hands, but he never releases me.

"Eventually," I say in that same voice my mother used to use when telling Kyra and I "maybe" instead of yes or no.

He smiles harder, more alluringly if that is somehow possible.

A maybe is never a yes, Aston. Didn't your childhood teach you anything?

His fingers ease their hold on me and he slides them down my arms slow enough to send a shiver racing across my flesh.

He likes it.

Why does he like every single little reaction that I give him?

Because he's a fucking creep, my rational mind screams at me while my distracted, irrational heart can't help but flutter when his fingertips tangle with mine before releasing me entirely.

"I'm an energy vampire. I feed on emotions instead of blood. And no one in Crimson City is as reckless with their emotions as you've been since you walked into this den of monsters just hours ago." The man looks at me like the Cheshire Cat. "So. Who. Are. You?"

An energy vampire. That explains why he knew I wasn't one of them within seconds.

I can deceive appearances, but I can't deceive my heart.

"Are there others like you?"

He shakes his head. "Eh, not really. I've only ever met one other in a pub in Rome." His flaming pink hair flips over his brow as he looks off with a reminiscent look in his pretty eyes.

I mean, not pretty. Puke green. Sickly green. Baby-poop green.

The kind of green the sea looks when poets and painters describe the waters just as the sun kisses the waves like God himself is touching the Earth with a little bit of Heaven.

Oh, my fucking God, what is wrong with me?

"Do you transmit your energy into others?"

"Aboso-fucking-lutely. You wouldn't even give me the time of day if I wasn't giving as much as I'm getting right now,

Six." His smirk is like sex and seduction with that disgusting word play.

And there we have it. He's using his powers to brainwash me into being attracted to him.

I sigh and look away from his hard jawline and overly defined Adam's apple. Since when did Adam's apples become so damn sexy?

When I became brainwashed.

Clearly.

I step out, gaining a few feet of space between me and my sister's tormenter. Then I study him for a few solid seconds.

He's six foot something. Lean muscle tone, but that means nothing to a supernatural creature with more power than any childhood superhero. What sticks out the most... is his band tee-shirt and scuffed black and white sneakers.

They say the worst monsters live among us in plain sight. Do they all wear tattered Riverdales tee-shirts and tattered skinny jeans too?

"People are dying here," I say casually.

His head bobs up. He eyes me skeptically, and suddenly it's a contest of who the real suspect is.

Shit!

What if I'm the monster, and Aston is nothing more than a lost man searching for his own feelings?

Too gross to consider.

That can't be right.

"The High Council of Crimson City has been dropping like flies," he says more harshly than I would have expected. "Croft Four, Victoria Korven, along with her assistant Rosalie Thames. And my own assistant just late last year. All three were disembodied slaughters of sex and blood. I've heard it's happening all over Chicago as well." His lips are curled as he looks at me, but not with that boyish charm he had just seconds ago.

But like a monster who truly does have hate hidden deep in his soul.

My stomach turns with disgust.

Something else keeps circling my mind.

"How did Victoria and Rosalie die?"

His jewel-like gaze searches mine. His teeth are bared far more than necessary, but he does answer the question.

"Just like the seven other human women this year. They were raped so brutally, Rosalie's right leg was detached from her body. Her neck was fed on so hard that her head was only attached by a tiny scrap of flesh. Victoria was in worse shape, we could barely recognize her. The human women got it far worse than that even."

This man's feelings, violence and kindness alike are a whirlwind of emotions. I don't think he even realizes it.

It's getting to me more and more as I speak with him.

A dampness stings my eyes, and I can't help but wonder if my sister suffered the same fate. But I can't ask a suspicious vampire how I died, now can I?

A deep flood of feelings drowns me all at once, and I look up again to find tears streaking down Aston's face. My hand lifts, and wetness meets my fingertips as I touch my cheek.

"You're crying, Kyra Vega," he whispers on a heavy breath.

I shove past him, my shoulder knocking his as I go.

"*So are you,*" I whisper right back.

FIFTEEN

Kira

I busy myself inside the small library in a chair that provides me with the perfect view of the staircase in the hall that leads down to the crofts.

One by one throughout the day, the vampires slowly descend to their coffins. Prey waits annoyingly just outside of the library door, like the perfect assistant and mate.

My reflexes kick up, recoiling at that last thought.

The list of things that keep me up at night are really growing out of control at this point. Prey being my undead boyfriend might just be the one that sends me over the edge.

Nicco helps Pavel down the stairs with his hand supporting the old vampire's elbow, and they stop just before they hobble down.

"Goodnight, Miss Vega," Pavel says with a perfectly rotten smile shining out through his dry, cracked lips.

"Goodnight, Pavel." I bow my head to him, but lingers a bit longer.

"It's nice to have you back. You do so much more for Rival's health than you could possibly know."

I pick apart his words and his demeanor, even as Nicco guides him back down the red-lit stairs.

Pavel has the appearance of a woman's worst nightmare, but I don't believe he has the strength to kill a high vampire like my sister or the others.

I flip open the first edition copy of Dracula I found and scribble a quick note about Pavel on the torn printer paper I have hidden inside it. It isn't much, but it's also only my very first day here. The real notes will get taken this afternoon, while everyone is sleeping.

But so far, it's not a bad collection of information.

<u>Acessa Milane</u>
Polite. But is she hiding something?
<u>Aston Cardence</u>
Has the strength and the arrogance, but his drive isn't there.
The boy has all the aspirations of a browning banana.
<u>Pavel</u>
...physically unfit.
<u>Rival Royale</u>
A lover is the first suspect.
He threatened me, twice.
Has the motive. And the ability.

"Are you writing... in a first edition!?" a horrified voice asks, and I snap my book closed on my notes as well as my pen.

I fling my head up to find Acessa with her mouth agape and her eyes wide with terror.

Wow. I really am the monster in this fucking church of villains.

"Um, no. I— Sometimes I just like to imagine what it's like to write a masterpiece."

She blinks at me.

"You're different from when you left for Milan." A soft smile pulls at her lips. "You were so quiet before. I like this change in you."

"Thank you. I'm trying," I smile back at her. Secretly. I'm listening to the ticking of the clock and wondering when she'll be tucking herself into her coffin for bed.

"I'm sneaking off to see Louis. Would you want to come along tonight?"

"Louis?" I ask with a pull of my brow.

If she could blush, it would be consuming the wide smile on her face right about now.

"Don't tell the others, but I've still been slipping out at dawn to go visit him. I really can't thank you enough for introducing us, Kyra."

Oh. That makes sense.

It also means Acessa could have a motive outside of the vampire's Council. Do the wolves hate them? Could Acessa have let Louis in?

What about Vuitton? Is he hiding something by keeping Creature Control out of this business?

No.

I mean... Shit, maybe?

I suppose I hadn't really considered him as a suspect.

"Of course, I'd love to come." I stand swiftly and hold tight to the book in my hand. "Meet you downstairs?"

She nods, and her short yellow sundress swooshes around her thighs as she strides out. Just for a different vampire to stride right in.

My jaw grinds when Prey comes up behind me. He continues to shadow me when all I really want is to hide the book away from the many watchful eyes lurking in this place.

It becomes painfully clear he won't be leaving. As if it's

nothing, I place the book on the lowest shelf, sliding it into a dark little nook that I pray no one ever stoops down low enough to admire.

"We need to talk," he announces to my back.

"We do, but not today," I try to walk away, but in the flash of a second he's in front of me, blocking my way.

His mouth opens, but the moment his gaze drops, his words fall away into something else entirely.

"You covered my mark." His attention never leaves my neck.

"I don't have time right now, Prey." I step around him, but he just flickers all over again in front me.

"*Prey!*" I huff.

"You're marked for a fucking reason, Kira." Sharp points of his teeth extend as he speaks low, with a growl lacing his words.

It's seething anger, and it grates suddenly against my already shitty feelings for him.

"And what would that reason be?" I ask, folding my arms hard across my chest.

"You know the reason why." His gaze narrows on mine.

But I won't let him gloss over this.

"No. No I don't. Explain it to me."

Say it. Say it. Say it.

"Because you're *mine*," he hisses.

And that's the fucking show, folks.

My finger stabs hard into his chest. "Listen the fuck here! I belong to no one. I'm not your fucking property, and I'm not your goddamn human pet to despise one minute and toy with the next."

His cold hand snatches around my wrist.

Prey's skin against mine does something strange, laying

claim to my erratic and confused little heart. The way he looks at me isn't possessive.

It's sad.

They've tagged this man as a low ranking vampire. A servant. He knows it would be an embarrassment for a High Council woman to bear his mark.

I'm not a high ranking anything, though. I'm just a girl wanting to put an end to the death count. I want to make what happened to my sister right.

And now I'm suddenly a woman who doesn't want to hurt Prey's feelings.

"I covered it because Kyra would have marked you a long time ago if that were an option. It would be too suspicious if I suddenly woke up with your mating mark and a human heartbeat to go along with it." My gaze flicks away from him, toward the floor. I still feel his attention burning over my features though.

His hand around my wrist is a strange caress now. Long fingers sweep back and forth along my pulse. It's a soothing sensation that reaches deep into my chest.

"I need a fucking cigarette," he whispers.

And then he's gone once more.

My eyes close. The air in my lungs slips out in a heavy woosh as I tread on with the bizarre nightmare of a life I'm currently living.

———

"Where are we going, exactly?" I ask as my high heel sinks into the grass for the fourth time in ten minutes.

Kyra would be absolutely pissed at the sorry state of her beloved shoes.

A chill clings to the air, despite how nice the sun feels across my face. Acessa leads me along through the tall grassy field without a single wavering of her steps. Somehow, her sunshine yellow wedge sandals are without stain or scuff while I nearly break my ankle with every misplaced step behind her. The morning laughter of small children and the rhythmic sound of the runners along the sidewalk of Lincoln Park faded away long ago. We've been weaving deeper through the trees and empty grasslands of the park for around an hour, and the hint of the cars and lives that fill this city aren't even a whisper any more.

It's just us, and nature. Suddenly, five enormous fucking wolves are lounging lazily in the bed of grass laid out before us. The tall grass is folded in on itself, pushed down and formed just right to create a fluffy bed for each of the five wolves.

The dark one of the pack lifts its head and immediately my heart stumbles as his eyes widen and his pointed ears perk up all at once.

Then he's running toward us at full speed.

The thumping of its paws mirrors my pulse. A growl of some kind rumbles from his throat as his big paws eat up the span of space that's safely between us and the monstrous beast.

Closer he comes. Faster.

He leaps!

And then in midair the shape of a man emerges from the fur of the beast and in less than a shaking breath he grapples Acessa to the ground.

A screech crawls up her throat and just as I take a step forward to pull the man off of her... Musical laughter, untamed happiness shakes out of her throat as he holds her to his chest and nuzzles his mouth into her neck. He whispers sweet nothings as he kisses her, and she just melts right into him.

It's Louis.

His lips seal over a black shape etched just behind her ear.

A crescent moon with patterns similar to mine.

A mating mark.

My mouth hasn't closed in several seconds and I'm not aware of anything else as I blatantly stare at the beautifully happy couple who haven't truly smiled once since I met either of them.

Until now.

"You came," a deep voice like warm honey calls out from over my shoulder.

My stomach flips at the simple sound of his familiar tone. I'm smiling like a giddy idiot when I turn to gaze at Vuitton's handsome face.

Oh. My. God.

And his mostly erect cock.

Why is his cock out? And why is it looking at me?

Shit. Why am I looking at it?

I fumble as I distractedly look away from the real monster among all these beasts.

Except, it wasn't really that big... *was it?*

I peek back down, just to look away even faster this time.

It definitely was that big, and I think it's still growing.

Just stop! Stop looking at it.

Stop it.

The rumble of Vuitton clearing his throat forces me to say something.

"Um. It's cute. *I mean—* I meant that *they're* cute. Acessa and Louis."

I hate myself so hard right now.

The delicious sound of Vuitton's laughter sends shivers of

awareness all across my arms, despite the oversized black coat I have wrapped tightly around myself.

"Sorry," he says. When I sneak another look over my shoulder, he's pulling on a thin pair of black boxers over the etched lines framing his hips. A good thing never lasts long enough, does it? "I didn't expect to see you for a while yet."

"Ever? Did you ever really expect to see me again?" I can't help but laugh, and now that I have the nerve to actually look at him the most warm and calming smile shines through in his pretty eyes.

"I'd have seen you again. I told you I'd be watching. I wouldn't have walked away without checking in on someone Kyra loved."

Why does my heart feel so funny? He didn't confess his love, he just said that he would do a wellness check. Calm down!

But I'm still smiling like an idiot.

Luckily, he is too.

"Want to see my burrow?" He changes the heart-fluttering subject with ease, and I am kind of curious about this burrow of his.

"Yeah," I nod and look back just once at Acessa to find her tangled up in the arms of her own very naked lover. "Yeah, let's go check out that burrow. Right now, before the wilderness gets a bit more wild over here."

Vuitton leads the way across the open field, the tall grass tickles along my fingertips as I follow him. The golden kiss of sunlight that highlights across the lines of his muscles is the kind of stuff sonnets are written about, I'm sure of it. His posture is hard and proper. I'm still stunned by his perfection when he lifts his hand and with the next step, the tall grass slips away.

Nature itself is folded down, criss crossing like architecture across the ground.

"You made this?" I turn, admiring the circular room he's created for himself among the walls of grass.

"Lie down," he says, and I don't know why my stomach dips at that command.

I kneel first, and then slowly lie on the soft blanket of bedding that he has made. It's warmer here. The wind doesn't touch my skin, and the sunlight soaks across me like it's peeking out from behind the clouds for me and me alone.

"It's comfortable, right?" Vuitton is smiling so hard I can literally feel his pride beaming.

"Incredibly so." I can't take my eyes off of the sweet smile he's lavishing down on me.

Until he too lies down, at my side. His arm brushes mine before he folds it behind his head and stares up at the soft white clouds.

I'm immediately too aware of our closeness. I'm all too aware of the last time he was this close to me. Our tongues were touching, he was just about to caress the neediest part of me, our entire beings were wrapped up in one another, and then we were so rudely interrupted.

I clear my throat hard and try to focus on what's important.

"Did my sister ever mention the vampire who turned her?" I ask.

An uneasiness shifts between us, replacing the erotic emotions that had recently swirled through me.

"Yeah," he says it so quietly that I can barely hear him.

"Who was it?" I ask in a rush as Aston's image flashes in my mind.

He shakes his head slowly, his attention never leaving the drifting clouds.

"She wouldn't say."

The apprehension and hurt he feels about that is clear in his smooth features.

"She didn't tell me either. Just... the details."

He nods. "We looked after her more closely because of it. She wasn't comfortable around men. She warmed to Prey quickly because they'd both been turned at the same time, but it took her a year to really depend on me. To trust me with more than just menial tasks."

I kick that thought around a bit.

"What about Rival then?" I can't help but wonder how she could never have mentioned a lover to me.

His rumbling laughter is so pure, I can even feel it reverberating in my own chest.

"Rival wanted to protect her. Men would test her. Male vampires of a lower rank tend to go mad when a woman is above them. So, Rival made it clear that Kyra was not to be fucked with in any way. He claimed her as his, but there wasn't anything there for him to claim. They were just friends, really. She didn't want any physical love, but she appreciated what he gave her all the same." His sigh is heavy, but reminiscent of better times. "I don't think there was anything between them but a ruse. He protected her by simply acting like a mate. Kyra would never take one though. She never even tried."

A comforting warmth sears through me.

Rival? The bitter Irish vampire with a cross too far up his ass? He was kind to my sister?

"That's sweet," I finally admit.

But then why did he react so ravenously drawn to me when he first saw me posing as Kyra?

"She had all these people around her who wanted to protect her, and yet none of us could." A thin line forms between his brows and I don't know why, but my fingers skim over his temple before smoothing the imperfections away.

Then he rolls over and turns away from his forlorn memories in the sky. He looks at me with a slow appreciation that I feel all over.

"I'm going to protect you, Kira Vega," he whispers like the vow is already set in stone.

It's unfair that I live in a vampiric house of cruel and crass men, but the sweetest man I've ever met isn't allowed inside.

I've even been claimed by one of them. My stomach does a flip at that reminder.

"How does a mating mark work?" The question sneaks out before I can stop it.

His lips quirk at one side before a big smile spreads across his lips.

He's so chiseled, even his jaw is a hard angle of perfection.

He's... so damn sexy. Sweet and sexy. How is that possible?

"For wolves, a mating mark is the ultimate goal in life. We travel in a pack of extended families, but we all crave to fill that one opening remaining in our lives. We want affection like most people want love."

"Aren't they the same thing?" I ask honestly.

"Affection and love? Oh no. Not at all. Our pack provides us with an unspoken sense of love. It doesn't mean that we like one another. And it doesn't mean we're kind and forgiving. But the mating mark, it doesn't guarantee love will be there. What it does mean is that one person will always care for us. Their heart is connected to our own, and despite any hate that might be under the surface, genuine affection will always find a way out. We just can't stop ourselves from being drawn to that source of feel-good feelings."

Feel-good feelings...

"You make it sound almost like a drug."

His laughter is warm and drips all through my chest until I'm smiling right along with him.

"Oh, it absolutely is," he whispers.

Vuitton watches me from the corner of his eye before rolling over again, and then his body heat is spreading across my arm in a tingling sensation of hyperawareness.

"Why do you ask about the mark?" His hand props beneath his head, fanning his honey blonde hair in the slight breeze as he stares down on me.

The thought of Prey and the wildness in his eyes creeps up in my mind once again bringing a heavy wave of uneasiness clinging to the memory.

"No reason," I say instead of word vomiting all my problems to this one man who already has more issues than he deserves. "How do wolves leave a mark if they can't feed the way vampires do?"

That sexy smile of his brightens until a dimple appears.

"They fuck," he says with a hard emphasis on the K, and I don't know why my thighs shift together at the sound of that dirty word on his sweet tongue. I don't know what he sees in me, but his laughter grows louder, shaking his whole body. "Some don't. Most supernaturals don't need any contact at all, really. I just wanted to see you blush. I love when your humanity shows."

I turn my head when I realize that I'm *showing*, and I try my best to calm that part of me. I'm supposed to be deep undercover in this world, aren't I?

When I look back at Vuitton, his gaze feels heavier against my skin. The sun seems to amplify the jade colors within the warm whiskey of his pretty eyes. And I'm all too aware of his attention when it falls from my eyes to my lips.

The breath in my lungs pauses, as if afraid it might be

seen were it to slip out. I swallow hard, and still he's staring like...

Like he just might kiss me.

Again.

A sharp inhale seems to cut off his trance as he looks abruptly back up to the sky and my heart finds its regular beat once again without all that attention making me squirm.

"It's a full moon tomorrow," Vuitton's hand lifts and he points to the pale moon peeking out over the morning sky.

"It's our birthday tomorrow," I shake my head hard at that foolish wording.

There's only one of us left to celebrate. Not that Kyra celebrated for the last two years, anyway. So now it's just *my* birthday. Not ours, we don't share it any longer.

His head turns back to me and those dimples are there at his lips once more. "It's your birthday tomorrow? On the night of a full moon? How old will you be?"

I nod, trying to shake the thoughts of my sister out of my head for a single moment of my day. "Twenty-One," I try to keep my voice steady when I reply, but it still dips a little anyway.

It really does feel like I've been alone without my other half for three years, rather than just a few short days.

"Twenty-One! You should have a wild party for a wild night. What do you want for your birthday?"

I look up at the perfect and charming man leaning over me. I have a nearly naked man alone right in front of me, yet all I can think about is Kyra's ghost.

She's all I ever think about these days. Her problems are my own now. They have been for the last three years, and if anyone really wanted to know what I want for my fucking birthday, it's to feel some kind of normal.

To live for myself more than I live for my twin sister for once.

At that thought, I study the faint five o'clock shadow kissing Vuitton's hard jaw. I follow the trail down to the curve of his chin and then over the soft line of his lips.

And suddenly my hand's there. My palm brushes over the course texture of his stubble while my thumb hovers over his full lower lip. His bright eyes remain locked on mine all the while.

I don't know when I lifted up toward him... but I'm just one bad decision away from pressing my lips to his and tasting that all-consuming euphoria I know he can give me so easily.

"What do you want, Kira?" It's the way he says my name that breaks my will. He speaks it like it's spelled heartbreak and remorse, one after another.

I know exactly what I want.

"I want to forget my guilt. I don't want to think. For a little while, I just want to feel."

His starburst eyes search mine. They hold me there, even as I lean closer and closer. Until his hooded gaze closes softly, and I press my lips to his and cherish every single heartbeat that slams in my chest without worrying that it might sound too loud, or too erratic, or too *human*.

A hungry breath slips between us just before his tongue claims mine. He kisses me deeper than the first time our lips met. He pushes for more, until he's all in. And both of us know, nothing could make us turn back now.

Fingers thrust through my tightly pulled back hair and he tears away my hair tie there. My locks fall across my shoulders and back down while his hand trails through the length of them, pulling at the ends as he goes.

He stares at me like he's thought about this for every day of his entire life, and now I'm finally here.

"Turn around," he growls on a breath before trailing a path down my throat with the warmth of his mouth.

My head tilts to accommodate him for only a moment before I shift beneath him. Long muscular legs become entangled with mine. The hard outline beneath his boxers catches my gaze before I can fully obey his order.

My mouth skims over his smooth shoulder and then the curve of his pectoral... down the planes of his stomach... down the thin trail of hair that leads further down, down, down.

"I said turn around!" Vuitton repeats on a ragged breath.

He says that. But he also lifts up from me, kneeling for me to gain access to any single glorious part of him that I might want.

Slowly, I slide out of my heavy coat and sit before him in just the tight red dress. I hold his attention as I too kneel, but in a more devotional pose. In a sort of way that bows *alllllll* the way down.

I lower my head even more, and his curious gaze watches me intently as I pull back the elastic waistband of his tight black boxers.

The thick dry grass blows in the breeze with a soothing sound of rustling. I know that we're concealed here... but anyone could just walk over if they wanted.

His pack could find us.

Fuck, they can probably hear us. Maybe even smell us.

But the need to feel what he's offering is more important than my modesty right now.

I pull the thin material of his underwear down until the thickness of his shaft wavers across my knuckles. A smooth rigidness teases my fingers, but I never fully caress him in the way that he's clearly desperate for me to take him.

My breath shakes over my lips as I peer down at the defined veins and the pulse that twitches through his cock.

As I stare, his big hand comes down. He coils his fingers around himself, not fully wrapping all the way around, then he strokes slowly up his shaft and ever so slowly back down.

"Is this what you want, Kira?" he asks in a voice like hot gravel.

My thighs shift with a sudden ache coursing through my center.

I don't answer him.

Instead, I look at him through my eyelashes and tilt my chin up to where my breath fans over his head. A thick drop appears beads there at the tip of his cock, and I watch him like a hungry predator as his lips part with a wanting breath.

And in my own way of answering him, I turn his question back on himself. "Is this what *you* want?" I ask with my lips brushing along his cockhead, his hand still working in that slow, torturous pace.

He nods roughly, shaking his golden hair around his features as he looks down on me with a new kind of desperation.

A desperation I suddenly like.

My lips part wider, and I can just barely taste the slickness at the tip as I speak. "I'm sorry, I couldn't hear you," I whisper against his flesh.

His jaw grinds.

"*Fuck!*" Vuitton hisses.

And then I part my lips just slightly to let his cock open my mouth for him. My tongue glides down his shaft with a pulse throbbing against me as I press against him.

A groan shakes through him and his hand falls away, but it locks into the messiness of my hair as he guides me further down his length. I take as much of him as I can, until he's brushing the back of my throat. And then I repeat the same motion all over again.

And again.

And again.

He grows impossibly harder against my tongue with every passing minute. The sounds of pleasure that rumble out of him are an animalistic growl that my sex reacts to instinctively.

He's making me wet just by hearing his approval.

I want him as much as he wants me, and I'm *so* tired of waiting.

"Turn around," he commands once more.

But this time, instead of waiting for me to obey, he pulls back from me and grabs my hips. I'm still catching my breath as he drags my knees across the folded grass and shoves my dress up and my lace panties down. The tight material of my dress bunches around my hips. My back arches for him. My legs shake at the simple thought of his thickness filling me. I wait for that first delicious thrust.

I wait.

I wait.

I wa—

And then the soft caress of his tongue flicks over my opening from behind.

A surprised gasp cuts over my lips.

His hold on my hips tightens as he begins to roll his tongue deeper, flicking over my clit before diving in as far as he can go. The shiver of his groan goes all through me as he tastes and fucks me with his mouth.

The quickness of it all makes every sensation blur into one. I can't tell what he's doing, but my body reacts to every single move he makes. Every lashing of his tongue is like a glimpse of nirvana that lights me up inside. He leaves me breathless and gasping and wanting and needing.

And then he stops.

My eyes flutter open to the intense sunlight.

The sounds of birds are suddenly heard around us. Or maybe they were there all along...

His nails sink into my hips and just as the world is starting to reform around me once again, he makes it all fade away. A slick hardness slides down my sex and across my clit.

My mouth parts. Then he teases my opening. My legs spread wider, but still he just brushes himself over my wetness.

I turn my head to look at him over my shoulder.

His lips curve up at one side in an arrogant *-how do you like it now?-* sort of way.

The cocky bastard.

Then he slides all the way in. Inch by glorious inch he stretches me to the most amazing feeling of fullness. He thrusts so slow that it's an awakening of his body entangling with mine. The most unstable shaking courses through me, and I don't think I've ever felt like this before.

"*Vuitton,*" I whisper and the groan he replies with just sparks all new tremors within my core that lash out all through my body.

My hands tremble over the dry grass, and my fingers dig in to find any source of stability.

But it isn't enough.

His hips collide with a speed I can't even imagine. It's fast and hard and I can't even focus on my own breathlessness as he uses my body in the best possible way.

"Fuck," he growls, and somehow manages to speed up his pace.

My moans are untamed as the winding whirlwind of pleasure inside me builds like a hurricane. Higher and higher, it continues to climb to new impossible heights.

His hand slides along my spine, and I'm faintly aware of

how hard he pulls my hair at the base of my neck. My throat angles and my spine arches for him as he holds me in place to fuck me deeper. His other palm pushes against my lower back, and that just makes every single thrust feel more intense and demanding.

It's... it's too much.

Wetness drips all down my thighs and across his cock as blinding colors like the sun and stars colliding together flash behind my eyes. Every part of me trembles: my legs, my arms, even my screams. The waves of the colors and emotions never fade as he continues his pace. They simply wash in harder with spirals of ups and downs consuming my body in deliciously addictive pleasure.

A growl and a curse rumbles over his lips as he thrusts in so hard it hurts, and then he tenses there. I feel his hold on me quiver just as much as his hips do against my body.

Warmth blooms in my chest, and I don't know why it feels so affectionate.

It feels utterly beautiful.

His fingers slip from my hair, and he drags those fingertips across the back of my dress in a slow caress of kindness. He leans over me and his big hands massage my neck before placing a series of soft kisses there.

Even after dirty, animalistic sex, he's still sweet.

I pull away from him and turn until my back connects with the cold ground. His warm palms slide up and down my calves. The color in his hooded eyes is a bright gold now as he gazes at me.

I'll never forget this. I won't allow my mortal mind to dull any of the emotions he just gave me. The way he made me feel, I'll never forget it.

But life carries on, with or without sentimental memories. I swallow hard as I pull my dress back down into place. My heart pounds, and only one thing is left clinging to the emptiness of my scattered thoughts.

"I really need to know everything you know about my sister," I whisper sadly.

Because even in all my bliss, her troubles are always at the back of my mind.

Vuitton nods quietly.

He searches around himself, and then pulls a pair of black lace panties from the ground. Without asking, he begins sliding them over my legs and up my thighs, putting me back together again.

"She never had a real relationship with anyone. She was close with Prey. They were friends of a sort, but I know there was a lot she never felt comfortable telling him."

That does sound a lot like Kyra. Vampire Kyra, anyway. My twin, the girl I grew up with, she was an open book.

But I guess that's just what life does to you. The dark parts consume all the good, and they don't leave any room for trust.

"Rival and her had a strange relationship, but he was even further behind Prey. She just... she didn't tell us things." Vuitton pulls on his boxers, but he never leaves his place in front of me. "I was her guard outside of the house, and she trusted me to be that for her," a line creases between his brows as he looks away toward the pale skyline.

The way my heart dives at the thought of his guilt eating him alive the same way it does me, I can't help but reach for him. My fingers brush over his knuckles and I sit up to truly face him.

"You're not responsible for this. Someone is, and they're still out there. They've done this to women over and over again. And they'll keep doing it, unless we can find and stop them first." I hate how hopelessly fragile I feel right now.

Exposed and raw to him.

I'll blame it on the sex, but really I know I'm getting too comfortable with Vuitton. I'm not ready to tell him my true thoughts or fears.

Whoever did this, they're not human. They're a monster.

A beautiful monster perhaps, parading around with a smile and charm that will kill anyone who mistakenly trusts them.

"In the basement, where they all sleep, there's a big metal door against the back wall." He looks me hard in my eyes as he speaks. "Take your finger and write *Kyra Vega* across the smooth plate there and enter slowly. You'll find more answers inside."

I blink at him. His admission leaves me stunned.

"How will I get answers there?" I ask as a prickling of strange energy tingles across the flesh of my arms.

But I never could have anticipated what he says next.

"Because the man locked inside will give them to you."

SIXTEEN

Prey

I feel like shit.

For years, all I've heard these fucks babble about is how lovely it feels to be in love. To have a mate.

Perhaps they should limit that fucking hallmark feeling to mates within their race. Because humans, they fucking suck you dry. I've never felt so much goddamn self-loathing in my entire life.

The council continues to murmur on about the cases of human women being found murdered in downtown Chicago.

"A young one. Only eighteen years old was found in the park last night," Pavel says as he sips from his glass of blood.

Nothing phases him, though. He's far too old to care much about the fragile mortality of humans.

"Eighteen," Acessa repeats with big wide eyes.

Rival shakes his head as he leans back in his chair, just to the right of the empty seat at the head of the table.

"Where's Kyra? This is the kind of thing that Kyra should be handling," Pavel sputters as he gets up from his place and starts wandering toward the door.

Fuck, I wish I could join him. Just walk right out and hope that the dead girl solves all our problems.

Jesus, Kyra would be able to solve all my fucking problems.

Like her sister claiming my mating mark.

The front door opens with a cool gust of wind and just a hint of the evening sun washes in across her long blonde hair.

Her... *messy* long blonde hair... Is that a twig in her hair?

"What— just what is that smell?" Rival asks with a scrunching motion of his nose.

Acessa smiles awkwardly, but rushes toward Kira's side.

"Let's go to your room," the vampire instructs with a pull of the stupid human girl's hand.

My eyes narrow when the scent finally hits my nose. It smells like mutt.

No, it smells like mutt and sex.

Then it hits me.

Something inside me flares up with anger and rage.

"You fucked Vuitton!" I announce to everyone from across the grand dining hall.

My words carry loud and clear, and even old man Pavel halts in his rickety steps. He turns, sunken eyes widen as he looks at her.

Meanwhile she just glares at me.

I can feel her hate like it's my own.

Because it is.

Why the fuck would I put my mark on a human?

Because I'm weak.

And I deserve a weak love.

My fingers dig into my palms at that painful thought.

"Keep your thoughts to yourself, Prey. I'll let you know when you're needed." Kira says, straightening her shoulders the way her sister used to.

"I *think*, you fucked a dog when you have a house of high vampires to choose from," I say flatly, the mark over my heart burning like a flame across my flesh.

How the fuck did a human mark me?

How could she even have that ability?

Her heels click loudly across the gray tile flooring, but she's in my face in the matter of half a second, glaring up at me with those intense gray eyes.

Kira's eyes are so different.

Maybe the others don't see it, but Kyra's eyes were the lightest shade blue. While Kira's are like the sharp edge of a blade catching the sunlight.

"You're getting fast," I whisper.

"And you're getting arrogant," she replies.

Her chest brushes mine, soft curves pressing into me while I go back and forth between wanting to claim her and wanting to kill her.

"Do not insert yourself into my life. You're an assistant. Remember that," she says harshly, and I can feel them all watching us.

I never would have challenged Kyra like this.

But I also wouldn't have marked my only friend, either.

The urges to hold her and to also shove her off a roof wrestle in my mind. She has to keep her appearance as Kyra, and I have to maintain my appearance as her assistant.

Not her mate.

And yet... I still can't stop myself from biting back at her lashing words.

My head tilts down until our breaths kiss, but our lips simply hover with just enough room for our abhorrence to be felt pressing against each other.

"Prey..." Rival warns.

But he means nothing.

Just like she does.

"I don't need a female," I whisper vaguely. "As a matter of fact, I'm immortal. I could easily just wait another hundred years for the next bitch to take my mark."

Her fierce gray eyes turn to slits as she glares up at me and the rejection I just fed her.

Fuck her.

And her mating mark.

SEVENTEEN

Kira

I'm storming down the stairs before he can say another word to expose us. My pulse is an insane thumping in my ears that beats so loud my skull pounds from it.

"Fucking annoying vampires, their magical marks, and their extreme bullshit!" I hiss as I round the last step and find seven ominous coffins laid out like décor.

What stands out the most in this moment though, is the solid metal door just behind them. It frames the display of coffins. Someone really put thought into the black glossy metal, directly behind the fourth croft.

Someone's in there? A man?

Someone with information?

I try to understand what Vuitton sent me here for, but I can't imagine a single soul on this Earth who would have details on my sister's death or the murders happening in this city. Yet I walk over to the center of the room anyway. A smooth metal plate is bolted in the middle. A soft worn spot reveals a lighter color in the center of the plate. Cold seeps into my fingertips as I settle my index finger onto the square and start to trace out a name I haven't written in so long.

Kyra Vega

The sound of heavy iron grating is all that can be heard in the silence. Unseen gears shift. I watch, but nothing moves as far as I can see.

And then…

Everything goes quiet.

I pause, but I can't stop my hand from lifting curiously to the cold surface. A pulse reverberates beneath my fingertips. Is it my own anticipation… or something else?

My palm makes full contact and I start to push hard. Power sparks to life in my veins. I shove harder, with both hands. I put my shoulder into it and I'm heaving by the time the door actually starts to swing open with my forceful steps inside.

Darkness blankets the room, but a blue electric light waves above the center of the closet-like space. It's a cylinder that illuminates from the ceiling to the floor. The beam of color moves continuously, like an ocean drifting out over the endlessness of the Earth.

"Someone new!" a pleased voice calls out from the shadows. "You have her blood, but not her eyes," an ominous voice says.

The voice circles the room in a terrifying way, and it's only then that I notice the door behind me has somehow closed.

Without a sound.

"Excuse me?" I say politely, but with an authority I don't actually possess.

"You entered the name Kyra Vega. I would have turned

you away, but your blood matches hers. So please, by all means, introduce yourself. I so rarely get new visitors." The voice is deep and warming now. Curious, but still powerful.

"I'd rather not," I say, still clinging to my humility.

"I'd rather devour your soul than have a chat, and yet here we are." Humor hums through his very creepy words.

"Who are you?" I ask instead.

Actual laughter, asinine amusement shakes through the room as well as the beam of light.

"You come into my confessional, and you have the mortal nerve to ask *me* who *I* am?"

I pause for a moment, but we seem isolated in here.

"You know I'm a human?"

"Incredibly, fragilely, *deadly* human." His gravelly voice purrs against only one of those four words.

"But you're not powerful enough to know my name."

A quiet chuckle is his only reply.

"Why do you call this a confessional?"

I edge around the bright blue wave of light and try to peer beneath whatever veil he's hiding under. Only washing colors of white and silver splay within the sapphire beam of light.

"Because that's what Zavia created it to be."

"She created you?"

That batshit crazy laughter cackles through my nerves once more.

"Hellfire, no!" he says like a snap of bones. "She summoned me. And then... she imprisoned me."

Summoned.

"So you're a demon?"

"You're a demon, 'Arry!" He mocks in a strange, high-pitched accent. "I'm a fucking Prince!"

Okay...

He is... an unstable asshole.

"Why did Zavia imprison you?"

"Tsk, tsk. Do not ask of others what you wouldn't want others to inquire about you."

...what?

"You can't tell me things about Zavia?"

"I cannot provide you with anything other than advice for yourself."

"You're a demonic advisor?"

"Aren't all advisors demonic?"

I blink into the light and wonder if he can see through to this side.

Why would Vuitton think that this psychotic demon could be helpful?

"You can tell me about myself. You can tell me all about Kyra Vega."

A beat passes.

"Very bold of a human, to try fooling a whole den of vampires, I like that," he whispers like a spider crawling over the dark wall. "But it's much harder to deceive a prince of lies," he adds quietly.

His voice sounds worn and broken.

How long has he been in here?

And how many people have used him like a thing rather than a conscious being?

"What's your name?" I ask.

I wish I could see him.

"I cannot give you my name. To give my name would be to give up my soul after I've already lost everything else."

My heart dips.

"I understand," I say gently. "I don't want to continue without... giving you value for your service to this council of vampires. You have value, and you should have a name."

That scathing laughter rakes out once more. "Humans

always try to be humane to things that don't need it. I'm not like you. I don't need your validation, I have my own."

"Okay." My words come drily, so I won't push that subject any further. "Tell me about the last time you saw Kyra Vega, My Prince."

The waves in the light halt. It all flatlines into a pale blue and I swear I can see bright eyes looking at me through the veil.

"Did you just call me your prince?"

I stare back at him, and the simple connection of our eyes is something I feel right down to my soul.

"You said you were a prince. Are you not?"

"I am." He studies me intently, making me shift on my feet and I wish I could see more.

But then the water effect ripples back in, and he washes away.

"Kyra Vega came to me on the last Sunday of October."

"October? She died in September. Is it common not to see her often?"

His throat clears softly. "They come to me when they need something. Information on humans. Death. Life. And they only come on the final Sunday of each month. No one argues for more time with a demon, I promise you that."

I attempt to make some sense of those rules, and try not to dwell on how sad that sounds for his existence.

Stop humanizing everything.

Focus!

"What did Kyra say that day? What information did she want?"

"She asked if vampires had an afterlife, the same way humans do." He pauses with a breath of laughter. "They don't, in case you were wondering."

"They don't," I echo.

"You can't live centuries upon centuries of being a heartless monster of the night and expect to get the same treatment as our dear, sweet Betty White." He scoffs in ridicule.

Why is he so bizarre?

Is it the isolation of solitude, or just the manic demon in him? I linger on the information, more than his strange behavior.

Kyra asked about death. Was she afraid to die? Vampire or not, she was still young...

And she was afraid.

"Did she ask about anything else? Say anything else? Mention anyone else?"

A soft hum of thought seeps through from his side. "The others, some of them babble on about their problems like I've got a demonic PhD to really help with their afterlife crises. Kyra didn't, though. She rarely saw me, and when she did, it was to ask very little."

I nod.

"She looked... sad," he adds.

"Sad?"

"She had walked in all poised with cookie cutter perfection, but by the end her lips always pulled so far down I swear she kissed the underworld a time or two."

"She was a vampire. She wasn't kissing hell, she was living it," I snap.

A rumble of laughter cuts through the veil.

"You pity her because you share her blood. But most vampires do not live through hell. They create it."

Tingles shiver up my arms.

The waves of the cylinder slow, and I find those firelight blue eyes staring at me once more.

"Thank you," I say before striding toward the door.

"Wait!"

I pause at the sound of his urgency. My head turns and I look into those intense floating eyes once more.

"She had a diary."

My brow lifts.

"You said she didn't tell you much. Why would she mention a diary?" The skepticism in my voice is clear.

"Maybe *she* didn't mention it. But I can't tell you that, now can I?"

Someone else read her diary.

And told a fucking demonic hostage all about it.

Why?

I'm flinging open the door in an instant and when I step out into the light of the croft, I come face to face with the most serious and stern look I've ever seen.

"Do not go in there again," Rival instructs.

What is with him? Does he just come around to bark orders and reassure everyone that the stick is still firmly in place up his ass?

My arms fold hard as I glare back at him.

"What have you found out so far?"

He adjusts his black sleeves along his fine suit, but he doesn't immediately answer.

"I'm still lookin' into it," is all he says.

"Well, what have you found?"

He looks away, but answers quietly. "I've found that Crimson City is not the place for us to speak freely. Like I said, do not visit with the demon again."

He starts to walk away, but somehow no matter how much of a bastard he always is, it always surprises me to see it up close and personal.

"Did you love her?"

I don't know why I ask him. Love has no place within a murder plot.

Maybe it can be a catalyst for the act itself, but no matter how much someone is loved, love will never be found within the act itself.

"I cared for Kyra. Very much," he whispers, surprising me with the rawness of his tone.

I'm still staring after him and thinking of how he kissed me just after he called me by her name as he walks away up the stairs.

He cared for my sister in some capacity. Someone cared for her, so she wasn't entirely alone here.

But I still hold so much guilt for not being here for her. I'm literally walking around like her own personal ghost in this life that she lived, and I carry that ghostly remorse with me.

Maybe I always will.

Even as I hunt her killer.

EIGHTEEN

Kira

I need help. I hate that I just admitted that to myself, let alone anyone else. But I need someone who knew Kyra to tell me what she liked, where she spent her time, and what she did here.

I find Prey still in the dining hall. His inky locks are shoved this way and that, but he doesn't notice me as he downs a full glass of blood.

Gag.

I keep walking. He isn't the help I need right now. He's the mess I need to avoid.

As a matter of fact, asking him any question would likely end in either one of our deaths or... sex. God, what if we fucked? Oh no. What if I liked it? Could I really stand to hate him by day and pray he finds my g-spot by night?

No.

Well... Maybe...

NO! For feminists everywhere, no!

But think of my poor, isolated g-spot. Do it for the orgasm. Do it for the O, Kira. Do it...

No!

I roll my eyes at myself and remember how Acessa offered to walk me to my room. Kyra's room. That would be a good start. Even if I can't ask her personal things about Kyra, at least she'd take me there. But how do I get her to make that offer again?

Shit.

I keep brainstorming as I wander upstairs. The lights are off on this side of the church, so it's getting darker as I walk, so dark I can't see where I'm going. But I suppose that doesn't matter much to supernaturals or nocturnal creatures who thrive in the night. My palm hovers over the railing to guide me up the last few steps and when I reach the soft carpet of the hall, my chest collides into something hard.

Something ominous and looming, and just close enough to make me stumble back... onto nothing.

My heels clatter over the lower step, but my weight pulls me back further. Gravity tugs right through my chest and the air in my lungs abandon me as I go down.

But then a strong arm wraps around my waist. I'm flung up in an instant, and my hands cling tightly to the soft cotton shirt I find myself pressing against.

Thrilled terror slams through me from the possibility of nearly dying, not by the fangs of a vampire, but my own mortal clumsiness.

Then... who's holding me right now?

I'm living in a house with an unknown killer, and right now I could be holding him close like some kind of savior.

I shove swiftly out of his arms and stumble away until my back hits the wall.

"I didn't mean to scare you," Aston whispers.

"You mean kill me? You almost killed me!"

A breathy laugh rumbles over his lips. "Well, you are a

vampire. A fall like that would hardly kill you... Right?" He asks me in a taunting way.

Like I might just slip up and confess all my secrets at his feet.

"If you're done being a passive aggressive ass, I'd like to go to my room now." I move past him, not even giving him a second glance.

"In the front house?"

My steps falter once more.

...the what?

I turn on the sharp heels of my shoes and really look at the shine of his eyes within the shadows. Even in the dark, he's all cruel lines and sharp smiles. Why are all these vampires so condescendingly cocky?

He holds my gaze, but never reveals his true meaning. Why am I doing this with him? I know he knows, and I'm ninety-eight percent sure my sister was far too smart to be murdered by an undead idiot like Aston Cardence.

So I give in.

"Front house?" I ask, despite my urge to feign understanding.

"Kyra Vega's room is in the back house. But you know all about that, right?"

My arms fold slowly, and I feel him follow my moves with a shift of his eyes.

How am I able to feel him like that? How is he so far under my skin that I can sense him watching me in the dark?

"Would you take me there?" I ask quietly, calmly and confidently.

"I'm sorry, what was that?"

A sigh shoves from my lips at the sound of his annoying voice.

"I asked if you would please take me to my room." I have

to really try to keep aggression away from my tone, but it's so damn hard.

"Sorry. It's so loud up here. Could you repeat that one more time?"

"I'm going to kill you!" I hiss.

"Ahhh, don't make promises, Six. I bet I'd like that."

I'm on him in the beat of a heart with my hands locking around the soft collar of his shirt. "What is your fucking problem? I've never met someone so fucking eager to die!"

Breathy laughter wafts over my wrists, and I can feel his genuine happiness flood through my body.

How does he so fluidly reflect every tiny sensation that he feels? It must be exhausting to compress everyone's baggage the way he must do it.

He doesn't struggle as he walks away, letting my hands fall around him as he slips out from beneath me.

"Come along then," he calls after me.

And like a flip of a switch, he's suddenly my ally.

For the moment, at least.

I trail behind him in the dark, when we get to the end of the hall, he turns down a section I haven't yet explored. Yellow light from an opened door glows into the shadows, and we step past the room without pause. I blindly follow this man I know nothing about, simply because he knows I'm not who I say I am. He's smart, and he trusts me, despite all my lies.

That doesn't mean I trust him, though. But it does mean I'll give him a small lead. I guess part of it has to do with the magic that's streaming through me now. He feels safe. His emotions are given freely, and if he had any underlying motives, I don't believe he'd be able to hide them from me.

I don't understand it, but my instincts do.

He stops somewhere in the middle of the long endless hall, and the door he stands before is large and overbearing.

He opens it with a swift and soundless pull. Cold air kisses my face and hair. He looks back at me with that same shine in his eyes as he nods and steps out.

The metal handle is enormous against my palm as I pull the heavy door closed behind us to find that we stand on a strange sort of bridge. White moonlight casts across the catwalk that leads from this building to another one across a courtyard.

The rear building.

Aston is quiet. For once. His steps are like a breeze, and he carries himself in much the same way. For an undead idiot... he is somewhat alluring. He maintains that same flawless veneer as the other supernaturals. It's an untouchable pull of the shoulders and lift of the chin.

As if fear or monsters don't exist in their world.

Except that I know they do.

Because otherwise, I wouldn't be here.

He pauses at the center of the bridge and rests a hand on the twisting metal railing. I watch him curiously as he stares out at the ground below. I come closer to the edge. I feel the bitter cold even more than Aston does, but I can't help but gaze down to try seeing what he sees.

There's nothing. Only shadows allude to the dark ground below.

What does he see down there?

"Come on," he says once more. Quieter this time.

Striding out into the night with the wind in my hair and the world open to me on all sides feels like I'm about to walk into the sea. It's as if nothing surrounds me, and there's nothing stopping me from going into the ends of the Earth.

Those weightless thoughts are pulled away when Aston opens the door for me and I hold his gaze for only a moment as I walk by. His eyes are brighter than I remember, they feed on me as he gazes.

And then I look away. This building is much newer than the church. An open corridor is alight with silver fixtures that hang overhead. Three are placed throughout the long hall. We stop directly beneath the one in the middle and Aston turns there to go up a flight of stairs. It leads us up to a tower-like landing with a single door.

"This is it," he tells me.

He steps back and gestures to my room. *Kyra's* room.

I turn the knob without hesitation and the space that opens up before me isn't at all what I expected. A writer's desk faces the only window. Pale green curtains just like the ones in our bedroom back home frames the view. Pens are perfectly in order to the right side of the desk, and a notebook sits in the middle.

Many notebooks lay on top of one another on a shelf on the side wall, but... that's it.

"There's no bed."

Aston steps inside, but only within the door frame.

"It's her room, not her bedroom. Each vampire on the High Council has their own space. Rival's is filled with collections of rare books he likes to display, but never read." His pretty eyes roll dramatically. "Kyra's was what she made of it. And I guess she liked to write? Or draw maybe?" He shrugs as he slips his hands into the pockets of his skinny black jeans.

"What's in *your* room?" I ask. Mostly because I'm not yet ready to open the notebook staring me in the face.

What if it says... something worse than the name of her killer? What if... what if she mentions me? What if she says what she really thought about our strained relationship?

I don't want to know about that, and Kyra wouldn't want me to.

"Um. Records, mostly. I picked a room at the end of the hall here. It shares a wall with Zavia and I know she's not a fan of... anything fun, really... so I don't get to listen to them much."

"She's gone right now though," I half ask, half state.

I look back at him and his dark eyebrows lift slightly. "Yeah," he nods, his pink hair fanning across his forehead.

My heart does a strange pounding as if even it's tired of me stalling.

"So, let's listen to them."

His eyes narrow on me, but for once since I've arrived here, it isn't a hateful look someone is giving me. It's one of confusion.

"Didn't you want to be here?" He lifts his hands to the small amount of personality in this tiny room.

The way he searches my features, I know that he knows. How? How can he know so much with just a glance?

My lips part, but my brain stalls without a logical excuse.

"I got the soundtrack from Underworld I haven't listened to yet." His strange statement hangs between us.

"What?"

The excitement in his smooth features makes me smile weirdly. "The movie. I found the soundtrack to the movie."

Still I stare at him, but my smile only grows.

"Why?" I can't help but ask.

"*Whyyyy?* Because every good vampire movie needs a little hate fucking, that's why!" His smile creeps up on one side, and it's apparent to me that my sister couldn't have hated him. He isn't the cruel man she described as her killer.

He's just a dork.

And she was just a broken woman.

Neither of them could see the other for what they really were.

His taunting with me is different than it was the first time we met. He wanted a reaction. He wanted to feed. I gave that to him freely, without even trying.

He wasn't an asshole, he was just hangry.

"Then let's hear it," I say, grabbing the notebook on Kyra's desk with one hand and his wrist with the other.

I guide Aston down the stairs and back to the floor we entered on.

I stop there and when I turn to him, he looks at me so much more intently. In fact... we're much too close. I stare up at him, our chests brushing lightly.

And then I step abruptly back.

"Which one's yours?" I motion to the doors, and it seems to take him a moment to realize I've asked him a question.

"Uh. Yeah. Right." He motions to the left, and I follow after him.

We pass a few open doors. Acessa sits on a pale pink mat through one in a downward position as she stretches her long frame. Her curious eyes pass over Aston, and then myself.

Does she know?

She simply smiles quietly.

Aston opens the door at the end of the hall, and he stumbles when he motions me inside. He's... excited, I think. And he's a mess because of it.

An adorable vampiric mess.

I slip inside his room to find a velvet blue chaise just in front of the large glossy window. Two shelves frame it on either side, both filled with records.

I turn in a slow circle. Gold and silver records are framed along all the walls, from singers and bands that have long since passed.

"How did you get all these?" I point, and a smirk kisses his lips.

"Well, I have visited a lot of mansions over the years."

I stare at him blankly for only a moment.

"You... you stole them? From celebrities?"

Aston scoffs dramatically.

"Celebrities are meant to be celebrated, are they not?"

"With petty theft? No, I don't think that's what their title means."

"I was quiet. No one even noticed. And if they did, they'll print themselves a new gold-plated record to gather dust in their empty condos. These ones are *mine*."

He filters absently through his shelves until he seems to find what he's looking for. The vinyl that he pulls from the sleeve catches the light of the chandelier with a black shine across the surface. He places it incredulously carefully on an antique turntable.

A beat of static silence passes before a symphony of music I couldn't recognize if I tried plays out for us. His eyes close as he sits on the edge of the chaise.

It has a nice beat, nothing wrong with it at all, But for Aston, it seems to send out a wave of calm euphoria that I can feel tingle through my own chest.

That's what music does for people. It provides us with emotions that we can't describe or explain.

And Aston lives for it.

Because he has so little of his own to hold on to, I guess.

"I like it," I whisper.

He nods with that pleased smile still ghosting his lips.

"Sit down. Read," he waves vaguely at my sister's book in my hand.

I take a seat next to him, our elbows brushing as I try to turn away to open the diary. My back leans into the chair with my legs tilting off just near Aston's thighs. He doesn't watch me, even if he is acutely aware of my every move. He just leans back against the wall and seems to lose himself in the melody. I know he's pretending not to care what's in this note-book. He's also pretending not to be aware of me.

All the while keeping me company. Distracting me if I need it, but giving me space as well.

My heart melts as I watch him avoid me entirely. He blatantly ignores me, really. He's better at it than most children even.

It's sweet, in an awkward way.

How could I ever have thought he was my sister's tormenter?

I take a slow breath in, despite my lungs protesting that there isn't enough space within the tightness of my chest.

Then I open the journal.

July 19th

Men are trash.

   Recyclable and reusable.

   But still terrible for the environment.

A loud laugh falls from my lips before I can stop it as I stare down at the short but adamant entry. Aston peers at me from the corner of his eye, but when I cover my smile with my palm he abruptly looks away.

I close my eyes as I imagine her painted red lips saying those few lines. She'd never! As a vampire, she kept our time together rather short and to the point. She asked about our parents, and myself. Short small talk that didn't really resemble the person I remembered at all.

But as my sister, she was always witty and funny.

And for some reason, this entry reminds me of that side of her.

Even if there was a darker meaning and reminder lying just beneath the surface of these inky words.

I flip through the entries until a more recent date appears.

September 1st

Confessing to Kira how hard life has been here was strange. It felt... painful to talk about it. I know I need to, but I guess after two years I'm still not ready.

Maybe I'll never speak his name to anyone as long as I walk this Earth, but at least I know he doesn't have the power to push me down any more. He can pretend all he wants, but we both know what he did. What he's still doing. I've shut my mouth and kept to myself here in Crimson City, but I'm not alone.

Kira still cares about me.

And someday I'll be able to tell her more than just a few small details about the man who took everything from me.

My stomach sinks fast and hard.

He used her and turned her and eventually killed her, and still that wasn't enough? He controlled her life here, too?

My memories of every single one of our meetings begin flashing before my eyes.

Kyra wasn't clipped and careless with our short time together. She was trained, and afraid to speak. To anyone. He took everything about her away.

Who was he?

Pavel? Rival? Aston? A member of Creature Control?

Who?!

I close the book for a moment, and I find myself holding it to my chest.

The same way I wish I would have held Kyra. I should have reassured her more. I should have tried harder. I should have told her she was loved and missed and...

"Are you all right?" A gentle voice asks just as a hand slips over my ankle and I realize I've pulled my legs up to my chest and basically used Aston as a footrest while I all but kicked him off his lounge.

"Oh," I try to move away, but he pulls back at my leg slowly.

My lips close softly as he brings my feet onto his lap and just looks at me with so much concern in his big, shining eyes.

"You can feel every single thing I feel, can't you?" I ask slowly as I understand why he's so good at knowing what I need.

Aston nods.

"Why does everyone hate you if you're so..." I lift my hands, but I can't think of the right phrasing. "Good at reading people?"

His smile is slow to creep across his face.

"Because human emotions are unstilted. Even the ones who try, they aren't very good at concealing their guilt, or rage, or their happiness. Whereas vampires won't give up those emotions so easily, I have to pry it out of them. Antagonize it out of them sometimes. Enrage it out of them if I need to." He smirks at those words, but I sense that it bothers him more than he would ever admit.

I nod, and he's absolutely right. I'm terrible at hiding myself here among these predators. Even the sweet ones like Aston. Which is why I need to be alone when I read the rest of these pages.

I slide my legs out from beneath his hands and stand up. "I'm going to finish this up in my room for tonight." He's nodding before I've fully explained, and I don't know why I'm smiling at him like a total drunken idiot.

"Can I show you why I think Kyra chose the smallest room the council had to offer?"

My brow lifts.

I hadn't really thought about it. I just assumed it was assigned to her or something.

"She *chose* that room upstairs?"

He stands, carefully pulling the needle from his record before slipping it into its dust jacket and back on the shelf in its proper place. He turns on his sneakers and an addicting happy go lucky energy seems to sway off of him. So much so that I follow behind him like a lovesick, record collecting groupie.

Wow. What is wrong with me? The guy plays one little movie soundtrack and suddenly my panties are begging to be tossed at his feet?

I shake my head and try to clear my messy mind as we travel down the hall and up the short stairwell once more. This time, he opens Kyra's door and joins me inside the small space.

"I used to spot her at night sometimes." He grunts out those words as he leans over her small desk and shoves the window open. Cold air breezes in, twirling my hair back from my face as I watch the strange man. "She'd be up here," he says as he climbs up, squats low on the table top and then leans out her window.

He stands up fully on the reading desk, his legs are still pushing off the edge of the white frame before... disappearing entirely. My gawking reaches a new level as the silence presses on, and still I'm just staring out the newly empty window.

"Are you coming?" Aston asks, his voice sounds far off, but I know exactly where the undead lunatic is.

"*On the roof!?*" I scream at him in a whisper. "No! No I'm not coming, Aston," I quietly screech. "Not all of us have an unbreakable nervous system. If I fall, I won't just bounce back up like your offensively durable ass would."

"*Offensively durable ass!* It is a rather nice ass, isn't it?"

"Come down from there!" I shriek.

"Come on up here!" He shrieks right back in an abnormally high voice to mock me.

I shake my head hard before placing the notebook back on the desk... and then climbing up myself.

This is so stupid.

Are we absolutely sure he's not a murdering psychopath?

Don't climb on top of a building unless you're ninety-nine percent sure he won't yeet you right off and call it an accident...

I'm... At least ninety percent sure... Ninety-nine, that's asking a lot, really. I don't even trust myself ninety-nine percent.

I tilt my head this way and that and eventually decide that a skinny white boy wearing tight black jeans and a "Golden Girls: That's my Type" tee-shirt is not the way I'm meant to go. He's safe. As safe as a bloodthirsty monster of the afterlife can be, anyway.

I cling to the top of the window as I slip my head out and shakily stand.

"This is stupid!" I hiss into the blowing wind.

My heels clatter just before I kick them off entirely. The scraping sound of them hitting the side of the building before falling out into the night claws at my nerves even more. Those were designer brands, but they weren't my style anyway.

Aston's crooked smile lights up his eyes when he looks down on the wet cat of a girl trying to cling to the rooftop.

"Come up," he whispers in a sensual tone that sends shivers all down my body. His hand extends and before I can awkwardly pull myself up, he's already grabbed my hips. And then my feet are no longer grounded.

An unsteady breath of a scream shakes through me, but as quick as the wind is against my body, so is he. My chest slides up over every part of him. He leans back to fully drag me up over the ledge, and then my breasts are pressing into his lean chest. Cold air heaves over my lips, and all I can do is blink down on the beautiful moonlit shine in the depths of his pale green eyes.

"It feels good, right?"

When he says those rasping words, I'm suddenly very aware of how my legs are spread nicely over his narrow hips. My body is melded into his like we were made to fit together just like this.

"The breeze up here, it feels good, right?" He tilts his head innocently at me and I realize with a slam of too many dirty thoughts that I'm the only one making this sexual.

Because he's a gentleman, and I'm the fucking pervert.

"Uh, yeah," I shove away rapidly but carefully from the safety of his arms. My ass hits the cold roof.

It's only then that I finally get a chance to look out at the view.

"Oh!" I whisper without a breath to hang on to. "It's beautiful."

Warm lights like fireflies shine out across the hidden city that mingles with Chicago like a hidden lover. The peaks of old houses and chimneys lay beneath the stars in an inky silhouette of shadows.

"I used to see her up here at night, when I would be heading to my room." He points down at the pale crosswalk below us. "She hated me, but I always thought that she was similar to myself. She was just better at handling it."

I tear my gaze off of the shining starlight city to look at Aston.

"Handling what?"

His lips part, but he doesn't immediately respond.

"Eh. The emptiness, I guess." His hands lift with vague gestures. "When you turn, your heartbeat slows. It slows down, but the world around you speeds up. Years fall off and away like autumn leaves on a tree. Over time, you can forget what it feels like to be excited about the mundane things. Like good weather, or warm sunlight falling across a morning chill. The smell of rain when it falls for the first time in spring. Amusements found in the tiny moments of life. All of that grows dull with time, and an all-consuming emptiness settles in their place."

The pain in my heart spreads the longer he speaks. My hand twitches to reach out for him. To remind him he's not alone in this world.

The way I should have reminded Kyra when I had the chance.

Without a second thought, my hand slides over his calloused knuckles. He turns toward me, but I look away the moment his eyes almost meet mine.

An intense melting warmth fills me up, and I just know it's coming from him. My energy is seeping into him, and he's feeding it right back to me. It feels genuinely good.

Distracting even.

Maybe that's why I try to focus a little harder, dig a little deeper.

"Did you ever see her arguing with anyone? Spending time with someone she clearly didn't want to be around?"

What am I missing in this chess game of a High Council?

"Just Rival. He was her only friend, and really, I could tell that they weren't really friends."

"They weren't?"

He shakes his head harshly. "Nah. Rival went out of his way to try to make everyone see him as her friend, even as her lover. But he was always pretending that there was more between them than there really was. The way she responded to a simple brush of their hands could tell anyone with eyes that she hated being near him."

He was always pretending there was more...

He can pretend all he wants, but we both know what he did...

My heart slams violently. Aston's comments swirl with the words written inside of Kyra's journal, and it's only then that everything comes crashing down into perspective.

Rival.

It's *always* the boyfriend!

Or in this case, the man who wanted so badly to be her boyfriend.

But instead, he just killed her.

NINETEEN

Kira

I'm stumbling through the window, out of the rear building and across the catwalk in a matter of minutes. My bare feet storm over the smooth tiles of the croft so rapidly that I can feel heat burning into the soles of my feet. But I don't stop until I'm in front of his door.

The metal plate is smooth under my fingertips as I hurriedly scribble out my sister's name.

I'm inside and rushing in front of the wavering blue beam with dwindling air in my lungs as I push myself to move faster.

"Did Kyra love Rival?" I blurt to the man hiding beneath the imprisonment of his curtain.

A pause dips in before an amused voice speaks slowly. "It isn't kind to speak ill of the dead," he says eerily.

I gawk with an open mouth. "It isn't speaking ill, now tell me."

"Why didn't you tell me Kyra was your sister?"

"Tell me!"

"Do not create dishonesty between us, Miss Vega," the demon says in a smooth threat.

"Kyra Vega was my twin sister. She was murdered, and now I'm here to find out who killed her, who killed the other members of the council, and who's killing the humans all across my city. Now, answer my question before he kills again!"

"You're afraid of this man?"

I want to scream. I want to claw into this bizarre blue shield that he's hiding behind and scream in his face until he reveals to me every little secret I know that he knows.

"He's a murderer. And every second you spend toying with me supplies him with more time to kill again!"

I came here with a flimsy little kitchen knife and so foolishly thought that would protect me from someone who even my sister couldn't fight off?

It's not enough against Rival.

"You want to know what I know?"

"Yes." I speak flatly through my clenched teeth.

"You trust me enough to tell you the truth?"

"Yes."

"I hadn't realized we were so close, Miss Vega," the demon says casually as the shine of his glowing sapphire eyes catches mine.

"Tell me who killed Kyra!" I fling my hand through the veil with tension splaying my fingers wide as I aim for what I hope is his throat.

But nothing except for cold ice stabbing into my flesh meets me on the other side. It prickles and stings my bones with vengeance. My scream washes through the colors, waving the blue and white and silver together like a building tsunami.

A calm touch wraps around my hand. His warmth burns through the cold, like numbing pain settling in.

"Our relationship requires blind trust, Miss Vega. A vow of eternal trust." His whisper washes over the back of my hand as a kiss seals itself there delicately. "Do you understand?"

A gasp cuts from my throat as tears openly trickle down my eyes.

"I trust you," I grind out. "Tell me," I whisper on a shaking breath.

I'll suffer through this pain. Even if this magic slices through flesh and bone, I'd be willing to sacrifice so much more to find Kyra's justice after all that I ignored when she was alive and needed me the most.

An unclear cutting smile lines through the water of magic that lies between the demon and I.

"A vow so deep should be commiserated," he whispers like a snake slithering through the shadows.

Hard breaths and desperate beats of my heart are all I can hear for a moment as I stare at him with pleading eyes.

"*Please,*" I whisper once more.

A cackle of laughter and the warmth of a fire burns up my arm as he pulls himself against me. Instead, I fall headfirst into the veil. A swoosh of magic fills my ears. Thousands of slicing sensations stab into my neck and face, yet still he pulls me closer. My feet stagger, but I fight him off enough to stay partially grounded.

The world around me is a colorless void of white, silver, and a hint of ice blue. And the man standing at the center of it is the same. His flame blue eyes stare curiously into mine. Messy hair the color of bright blue gemstones hangs over his brow as he looks down on me with a hooded gaze. Tall white horns rise up from his temples in a terrifyingly beautiful arch.

"You're powerful, for a human," the demon whispers strangely. "Bewitching too," he adds. He speaks like he's afraid he might break me if he leans any closer.

Yet he does. He leans down, his hair skims over my cheek as his breath tingles over my ear. "Most delightful of all," he pauses as he gazes at me from the corner of his mischievous eyes, "your soul is now a part of mine!"

And then he slams his lips into mine.

He tastes like Hell and candy. Like smoke and sugar. Like a deadly, deadly mistake.

I pull back from him, my hands clutching onto his as I shove him away. My palm snaps across his cheek just as my knee comes up fast. My foot connects with his groin, but he grabs me there. He holds me close and as I stumble back, he follows.

My ass hits the floor with a thump of discomfort slamming all through my body as his heavy weight collides into me. His smooth chest glows in the darkness. Symbols like nothing I've ever seen before slash over up his arms and down the center of his chest like a glowing neon sign. Black, tattered pants cling to his waist where even more swirling letters dash down the hard lines of his hips.

Color kisses his pale skin now. But oddly, his eyes and hair still retain that shimmering gemstone color. He holds himself up with his arms braced on either side of me as he stares into my eyes like I'm the most enchanting thing he has ever gazed upon.

"Tell me!" I repeat once again on a ragged breath.

I don't give a single fuck about this demon. I don't care that I've released him without a single understanding as to how or why.

He made a vow, and now he's going to tell me everything.

Right now.

"Kyra didn't love Rival. Rival felt guilt toward Kyra, and she chose to put up with him for some reason." He speaks factually as his fingers brush my hair back from my face.

I bat his hand away.

"Did Rival kill her? Did he? Tell me!"

"I only know what people tell me. What they ask of me."

I blink up at him.

No one's going to flat out confess. I understand that.

I get it.

I just—I need more answers.

"Rival once asked me where to hide a dead body. And about the best way to cover up a murder." The demon sits up slowly.

My hands shake across the cold floor as I push myself up as well.

"He buried someone in a used grave just between the front of the house and the rear. And then he bought time to avoid any investigations." He tries to search my face as he speaks, but I'm already standing and running for the door.

Kyra's here! Her body was just carelessly buried on top of a stranger's. And the man who brought me here to help her, he's really just hiding her for as long as possible.

TWENTY

Kira

My bare feet fly over the floor so fast that the sounds of cracking floor tile calls after the wake of my footfalls. I'm up the stairs and rounding the door to Rival's library room in mere moments. The old books are perfectly in place along his floor to ceiling shelves. A half empty glass of blood sits abandoned on the fireplace mantel.

And the book I tried to hide so carefully lies open to my scribbled note of paper on his desk.

Acessa

Polite. But is she hiding something?

Aston Cardence

Has the strength and the arrogance but his drive isn't there.

The boy has all the aspirations of a browning banana.

Pavel

...physically unfit.

Rival Royale

A lover is the first suspect.

He threatened me, twice.

Has the motive. And the ability.

The signs were all there. I just didn't recognize them in the man who was supposed to care about my sister. Even more innocent people have died because I refused to see him clearly.

And every second that passes is another opportunity for him to strike.

I stride out of the empty room. My chest collides hard with someone else.

"Slow down!" Prey looks me up and down and though there's hatred in the hard pull of his brow and lips, his gaze is soft as he apprises me. There's love and concern written all over his moody little face.

I just don't have any time to care at the moment.

I shove past him, but he grips my wrist and pulls me close.

"We need to talk," he says.

"I have to go." I shake him off, but still he clings to me.

"I just. I'm sorr—"

"Rival killed Kyra!" I shriek just to get it through his thick skull that something more important than his arrogant feelings is happening right now.

His mouth falls open hard. "*No*," he whispers slowly.

It's only then that I see Prey for who he really is. He's been belittled and shoved down by all these superiors... and yet he continues to trust them without question. The confusion and disbelief in his features tells me I'm threatening the foundation of his existence here.

And I know he won't be the only one who feels that way if I call Rival out.

Will the High Council stand by his side? Will they cover for a murderer? A rapist? A monster?

Prey is still staring at me with wide, uncertain eyes when I slip my hand out of his and keep going.

I'm through the quiet dining hall in a matter of seconds. Acessa's assistant, Blyke passes a look my way, but he doesn't comment on my messy hair or dirty feet as I search the room. He eats alone, but there's something else about the young vampire...

Every drink from his wine glass is a stiff and proper motion. A nervous tension expels from him in waves that I can feel in my own chest.

Why do I sense him in that way?

Whose magic is bouncing around me at this moment?

I shake the thought away, but before I dash out of the room an even more nervous voice rings out in a stutter.

"Y-ess, there have been two more human murders in the Chicago area, Ma'am," Pavel says with a shake of his frail hand as he walks side-by-side with a tall, regal looking woman.

Her fiery hair is so vibrant that it matches her tight red dress impeccably. Her smooth pace and the casual click of her designer heels steals all of my attention.

Councilwoman Zavia!

Her piercing gaze zeros in on myself as well.

"Have there been any more within our walls?" she asks in a flowing velvety accent.

"None within the Crimson City. Creature Control have not been allowed within here without your approval, Ma'am." Pavel too pauses his thoughts when his attention falls on me.

"Where are your shoes, Vega?" Zavia asks as her stare becomes rather deeply concerned for my black and dusty feet.

My toes lift and scrunch awkwardly as if I can hide them away somehow.

Do I say it? Do I out Rival? And say what, exactly? That

he killed me? What would they do to a human snooping around their High Council?

"I found out my favorite red bottoms are a fake. I'm boycotting until I can make a trip back to Italy myself." I flip my tangled hair back from my face, and it's then that I realize I'm sweating bullets.

I'm burning up, actually. I swipe at my brow and moisture appears along the back of my hand. Not only that, but... Two small but solid points poke out from against my temples.

Are those... Are those horns?

Fuck.

What in the name of Lucifer is happening to me right now?

Don't *act human. Don't act human. Don't act human.*

My lips tremble, but I shove a stiff smile in place.

I turn, and swiftly but casually stride out of the room.

"Vega?" Zavia calls after me.

I walk faster.

"Vega?"

And then I'm running.

Her yell echoes after me, but everything passes by in a streak of dark blurring colors. I don't even consciously think about where I'm going.

I just run. I keep going for so long that the stuffy warmth of the house falls away, and cold night air kisses my face.

Damp grass flicks along my ankles as I walk, slowing my pace the moment gray stones come into view. Hundreds of them are spread out before me beneath the light of the full moon.

One of them belongs to Kyra now.

She's buried here in a used grave. She's been laid to rest among so, so many forgotten tombs.

But ultimately, she's all alone out here.

My heart is so warm it feels like fire within my chest. That warmth falls low and hard as I think about everything Kyra went through without me. Without anyone by her side.

I thought I came here searching for her killer. Maybe I was really searching for her.

Like I should have done two years ago.

My knees give out and hit hard against the wet ground. The breeze picks up, but no matter how much it flings my blonde hair across my face, I can't see anything except the darkness surrounding each and every pale stone.

"Get up, Miss Vega!" A deep tone commands.

I blink away the wetness in my eyes, but I remain seated in a heap of too many regrets.

A smooth shoulder bumps against mine as he slides down against my side. And then the Demon Prince is also kneeling in the dirt beside me.

"You didn't kill her," he whispers.

I shake my head slowly and a wetness splatters over my cheeks. I peer up at the heavy gray clouds hanging among the bright white moon.

"But you know who did." I feel him staring at me. "You're powerful, Miss Vega," he whispers manically against my hair.

A shiver shakes through my core as his hot breath trickles down my neck.

"You know who killed her," he repeats as he pushes back my hair behind my ear and whispers intimately, like an ocean breeze caressing my skin. "So get up and fucking annihilate the man who hurt her! Who hurt you."

My feet push up and I'm standing just as the rain pours down over me. It soaks through my dress and even the deluge of cold water doesn't cool my burning flesh.

I look up at the dark sky. The beauty of it is all around me, but I can see is him instead.

Aston sits on the roof and watches over me like an angel who knows what sin I'm about to commit. He knows me deeply. I feel him in my mind like a calming thought among all the chaos.

He feels *good.*

He's the encouragement I need right now. Even as I turn toward the front house and spot a true monster within the night.

Rival Royale comes forward out of the darkness like a shadow coming to life. He holds something sprawled across his arms. His black suit is stained with a darker color across his chest and sleeves. That's because he's covered in Acessa's blood.

She lies limply in his arms, her head has fallen back with her mouth hanging wide open. Her long arms dangle against him, jostling with every step he takes. His dark eyes meet the rage in mine.

"You killed her!" I seethe.

He shakes his head slowly.

"I found her out front. She was facedown just two yards from the steps of the house." He keeps talking, but his words are an empty sound within my mind.

The excuses he gives for Acessa don't register.

Instead I cut him off.

"How did you kill Kyra!?" My flashing eyes burn into him so hard it feels like pure hellfire sizzling through my skull.

His dangerous gaze narrows as he carefully lies Acessa on the ground like she means nothing to him. Like she *is* nothing.

"How did the demon get out?" He looks over my shoulder at the man I feel standing just behind me.

"There's a demon out?" The Demon Prince echoes with exaggerated terror.

But I don't dare look away.

"Was it an accident? Why kill her two years after?" I step closer, water seeping over my toes from the puddle that's growing with every heavy drop that falls from the sky. It drenches and cools me, despite the heat that's flaming wilder within my chest.

"I didn't kill her!" Rival growls out.

"You're a shitty liar!" My fingers dig into my palms, nails biting into my flesh one by one. "You killed her, and you'll kill me the moment I'm not of use to you. You fucki—"

His weight crashes into me. Water sprays up around us as he pummels me into the grass.

"Stop talkin'," Rival grinds out through his clenched teeth. His hands dig into my wrists as he brings them up high above my head. "You're fooking reckless. Your research, your fooking words, even your fooking pussy is reckless! Mating with men who have no use for a human." He shakes his head hard, casting drops of cold water across my cheek as he bites his words out an inch away from my face.

Slick fingers dig into my hands, but still I shove against him, fling him off just for him to come right back down with the strength of ten men binding me in place. He's like a force of gravity all on his own. He outweighs me with far too much power. It's too intense. Too much...

The snapping sound in my wrist sends a shrieking cry hurling up my throat as tears stream down my wet cheeks.

And then he's gone. The press of his hands locking over mine is jerked away and the splatter of mud across my neck is felt just as Rival crashes into the earth.

"Don't you ever touch her like that!" Aston growls in a dominating tone I've never heard before just before his head slams down. Another cracking sound echoes through the air as Aston's skull crashes into Rival's.

Both men groan, but Aston retreats with a flash of blurring colors. "Run!" Aston waves me off as he watches Rival slowly stand with newfound anger lining his face.

I peer around. The demon sits on a worn grave with his palm under his chin as he animatedly watches me. Prey stands at the door, rain washing over him as he looks from me to Rival and then back to me again.

But he never takes a single step forward.

He won't claim me. And it's clear where his loyalty lies.

My body shakes as all the fiery coals burning through my veins fire up at once.

"I suggest you step back, Mr. Cardence," The Demon Prince instructs as he picks distractedly at his manicured nails. "Miss Vega has a vendetta to appease. You wouldn't want to get any blood on those fine skinny jeans of yours." His lips curl as he looks up at Aston's apparel. "After this, I think we'll be in need of a new wardrobe. Miss Vega, once you've disposed of Mr. Royale, can we go shopping?"

"It's late. The stores are closed," Aston answers breathlessly like, that's the real problem at this moment.

"Shut up! All of you!" Rival points at the two of them, but keeps his gaze locked on me. "I didn't kill Acessa. I wouldn't have hurt Kyra! I—"

"Don't you dare say you loved her." The pain in my wrist is numb and forgotten as I take a step closer.

"I didn't," he whispers, the moon light gleaming in his steely eyes like a deadly weapon.

And I can't listen to another word out of his fucking mouth.

I don't feel anything. The air in the night is gone. The rain disappears. Everything falls away as I move so fast my body never takes a single step, but I disappear in a mist of shimmering crimson colors. Then I land with my hand around his neck in the very next instant. My nails sink into his throat as I lift him ever so slowly from the ground. His shoes kick against my shins as he rises over me. The light of the moon creates a halo around his handsome features. I don't know why my heart dips and dives and burns as I stare up at him with far too many emotions coursing through me.

"*Kira!*" Rival grunts, and the simple sound of my name feels tainted and scarred against his lips.

He was supposed to be her friend.

Wind twirls around my feet as they lift just slightly off the wet ground and I bring the two of us air borne in a way I can't even explain. His hands wrap around mine as I squeeze harder against his windpipe.

We levitate higher. Then I fling him down and I'm on top of him in a matter of seconds. My nails poise over his dirty suit jacket. Before I can press into him, his leg comes up fast and hard. He tangles around me. Pain sears through my skull as I hit the ground head first.

A slick hand shoves up and around my throat so hard that I'm staring up at the steeples and spires of the church, gazing up at the stars that paint the night sky beyond. His other hand slams over my lips and when he comes back into my view, giant black wings rip out from the back of his suit. They tear through the cloth and his black dress shirt falls away as inky lines of smoky tattoos and eerie red marks of color kiss his flesh here and there.

He truly does look like a storybook monster. And it appears that I'm to be his next victim.

His slick body lowers over mine, his chest pressing into me in a familiar way.

"Don't ever fooking insert yourself into things you don't belong in!" Rival seethes against my neck like a lover's promise. His hold around my throat tightens.

My lashes start to feel very heavy.

His body against mine is a strangely calming weight. My eyes close tiredly, but my heart continues to pound with reckless determination.

My hands cease clawing at his flexing forearms.

"Why aren't you helping her!?" I hear someone scream.

"Because she doesn't need us," a lazy, distracted voice answers. The sound of that warm tone ignites memories within me. He's someone I've known for several lifetimes over. His smile and laughter rings through my mind, lighting me up with mementos of love and lust.

A memory drifts in of my Prince tangled up in white sheets that match the color of his horns. His hands are around my waist. His body is smooth and hard against mine as he lifts my thighs and wraps me nicely around his hips. His mouth is hot against my neck, my shoulders, and my breasts.

The warmth of his body and the blaze of our kiss fades out.

"Get up, Miss Vega," he growls lazily from somewhere in my mind.

My lashes flutter, and I look back up at the crazed vampire leaning over me. It's a conflicting feeling, even as I know what I'm about to do.

I don't want to hurt him, I thought he was my sister's protector.

But I won't hesitate, I'll kill him for everything he did.

My hand flings out, and it's like I knew where I left it all along. Or maybe my senses are better than I realize. Damp grass slides over my fingers before I grab the sleek object around the middle like a makeshift weapon. The red bottom of my stiletto is in my hand in an instant and fling it forward, hard. His scream accompanies his thrashing as I sink the pointed heel deep into his neck. His black leather wings spread wide, but never lift him up. Dark blood trickles out as his fangs flash out with a gravely hiss.

His teeth drag across my throat, but I hold him back.

Just a little longer!

His mouth is hot across my flesh and his teeth are sharp scratches that keep scraping closer and closer.

Until...

My hand comes down hard once more. A cutting breath leaves his lungs and blood slides down my fingers as the heel sinks deep into his chest.

Just over his heart.

His shining starlit eyes stare down on me.

"*Cuishle,*" he whispers oddly.

My heart stumbles as I gasp for a solid breath for the first time in what feels like an eternity. And then I shove him off. He hits the ground at my side with a heavy thud.

Gentle hands wrap around one of mine and Aston steadies me carefully as he pulls me up against his side. His hands hover around my face, but he doesn't touch me.

He's always so careful. So aware.

So...

I wrap my arms around him in an instant and he lets me. He holds me hard, and my body sings from the feel of it.

I just killed a man.

I'm a literal vampire slayer.

And all I want is to be held for a little while.

TWENTY-ONE

Kira

"You tried to kill a High Councilman!" Zavia's red lips purse harder and harder every time she speaks. "You're lucky I don't deal with you personally!"

Pavel and his assistant Nicco stand quietly behind Zavia. Prey kneels before me and attends to my wounds with a wet cloth. He doesn't try to meet my gaze, not even once. He keeps his attention averted in a respectful way that eats at me with each passing second.

"You're lucky I was able to get to Rival before the blood settled in his heart."

My teeth grind.

"You saved a killer then." I square my shoulders as I look up at the one woman I was told not to talk to.

"Rival Royale is no killer." Her deep green eyes blaze with authority.

"Acessa is dead!"

"We do not know what happened between them tonight."

"We will by dawn," I say and Prey's hand pauses. His

pretty gaze drags slowly to meet mine. "I called Creature Control."

Zavia's eye twitches.

Pavel looks to Nicco and I hear the young man whispering loudly to repeat what I just said. "Kyra called Creature Control to investigate the High Council."

"Oh, Zavia will not be happy about that," Pavel announces so loudly that Zavia's eye twitches all over again.

Aston's lips part and I just faintly hear a curse whisper out from the corner he leans in.

"You called Creature Control?" Her voice lowers to a deadly tone.

"They'll be here at sunrise to collect Royale." I don't know why I challenge her so hard. It feels good though. It feels good to force justice into this world where they were so happy to just toss a victim into a used grave and forget about her entirely.

I won't let that happen, though.

Zavia's jawline tightens as she swallows hard before turning on her high heels and storming to the stairs.

"And someone go find the Prince! I leave this house for one week and literally all Hell breaks loose!" Her young assistant chases after her, scribbling notes furiously in a little worn notebook.

Nicco holds out his hand and assists Pavel into croft number two. The old vampire is laid to rest and Nicco seems relieved once the lid to the coffin is finally in place over his master. Nicco's heavy sigh follows him as he too heads upstairs.

Prey continues to wipe the dry blood from my hair, but a new and familiar scowl is lining his face.

"You're an idiot for attacking him," Prey grunts as he runs the cool rag delicately across my cheek.

"She's a badass," Aston says with a smile.

"Can she still be a badass if she's dead? Because that's what Zavia will do to her if Creature Control investigators riffle through our house and Rival turns out to be innocent." Prey's head shakes back and forth like the good little prep boy he is.

"And you'd rather she died without a fight in the cemetery? You'd want to bury her just like you did Kyra?"

My mouth falls open.

"You buried Kyra?" I ask, gripping his wrist in an instant to stop him from his busywork with my fucking face.

A scent like smoke and sugar explodes right next to him. The vampire lashes without thought. His fist and wet rag collide with the hard jaw line of a mysterious demon prince.

"Yes, do tell how you buried Kyra in a used-up hole in the ground without so much as a goodbye Lassie from her family." My Prince leans against the croft I'm sitting on and rests his head against his hand, ignoring the light trickle of blood slipping from his lower lip.

"Stop trying to get Kira to kill me next," Prey whispers with a hard pull of his down turned lips. "Rivale asked me to bury her. And really... I didn't like the idea of someone she didn't trust placing her in her final resting place.

"*Final resting place*," My Prince mocks in that high-pitched girl voice he likes so much. "As if any of you ever rest. Even after death." He rolls his bright blue eyes so hard I'd swear he was demonically possessed if he wasn't already demonic royalty.

"I believe you," I whisper suddenly and all three of them snap their attention to me. "What? I do."

"Why?" Prey asks on the quietest voice.

My heart kicks up as I look at him and the cruel disbelief lining his face.

"Because you're my mate and I know when you're lying, Prey," I say.

His Adam's apple bobs as he shifts his attention to the ground.

A tension pulls tightly between us and all I want is a hint of decency between us. Mates don't have to be lovers. But I truly want some form of friendship with my sister's closest friend.

She trusted him.

I want that for us too.

"Being someone's mate doesn't mean anything, Pretty Human." Prey tosses the rag down at my side and strides away from me.

"You're afraid," My Prince speaks loudly and clearly, letting his accusation crawl the walls around us. "You're afraid she'll never want you just like everyone else in this fucked up little society. Humans are beneath them but vampire's assistants, they're just barely above humans, aren't they?"

"Wow. Demon man woke up from imprisonment and chose violence," Aston says under his breath.

"You don't know what you're talking about." Prey levels his stance in front of the demon and I just know the two of them will end up with more fists thrown if we're not careful.

"If you're not afraid," My Prince tilts his head slowly with a smile carving up his face, "then kiss her."

"Wwhat? I'm sorry, what?" Aston interjects and it's the first time I've ever seen him stunned.

And I agree.

"Our lives are not a RomCom for you, DP. I'm so sorry." I fold my arms as I look at the demon but for some reason snickers, actual snickers of laughter, are shaking out of him.

"Did you just call me DP?"

"You won't tell me your name. I'm just going to have to go with Demon Prince and that feels incredibly weird to say."

"And you thought DP was the better option," My Prince says and all three of them are giggling like a lunch line of little girls.

"What is the big damn deal with DP? What?"

"Nothing. No. I love it. Definitely call him DP. It's just penetratingly accurate is all." Aston's nodding harder and harder.

What?

My eyebrows lower but I still don't know what their issue is.

"Can you—do us a favor—please ask for DP. Just like in a voice that says you're parched and maybe in a little bit of pain but like a good girl pain, you know?" Aston hangs on my silence as I glare at his weird fucking request.

"You're such an undead idiot," I finally say and Prey and DP both nod in agreement.

How did I get sucked into the lives of such strange and messy men?

"It'll strengthen both of you if the mark is accepted," Demon Prince says after a moment of casual silence settles in where mocking laughter once was.

Prey's head snaps up and he looks at the demon for several seconds. He doesn't believe him.

Or maybe he really is afraid. What if I lower his power instead of increase it?

"She has a vampire's mark, a wolf's mark—"

I cut him off hard. "A wolf's mark?"

He rolls his eyes as he lifts my hair and points to something at the back of my neck.

I touch but feel nothing there.

...I swear if I marked on Vuitton too... Two of them? How

could I have marked on two men? It's like the fucking zombie apocalypse. They just keep infecting me. And I keep going right back like more dick might be the antidote.

"And now," DP continues as I'm still rubbing at the back of my neck, "the magic of a demon is in her heart. You're a fool if you think she's weaker than you." My Prince remains impassive in appearance but I know he's invested in this.

Why?

"You gain power when I gain power." I arch an eyebrow at the demon.

His smile broadens. "You're clever, Miss Vega."

Prey turns and there's a question in his searching eyes as he looks at me.

Black smoke blooms all around but then the demon's closer to Prey than he was before, his face just an inch from the vampire's.

"*Kiss her,*" he whispers like a dirty little thought.

Prey steps between my thighs and I let him. Curiosity prickles through the room like a crawling, needy parasite. Prey leans in and I'm drawn to him as much as he seems to be drawn to me. His lashes lower.

My gaze lifts.

And I lock eyes with Aston as Prey grips the back of my neck, and seals my lips to his. Red burns into the whites of Aston's eyes as he holds my gaze. My tongue slides out to meet Prey's and I can't help the moan that shakes through me as Aston licks his lips and Prey kisses me harder.

Sparks burn through my veins.

Prey's mouth lowers and the warmth of his tongue rolls over my throat. Sharp teeth scrape over the mark I know is just beneath his lips.

His mark.

"Lie back," Prey orders and my hands shake as I lean back

against my elbows before lowering my back to the hard lid of my croft. "You smell so fucking good." His breath fans across my thighs as his head disappears between my legs.

My Prince flicks his sapphire eyes slowly over my body before meeting my gaze.

"What are you thinking?" he asks in a mystified, far off voice.

Fingers lock around my panties and the drag of lace over flesh makes me shift in place.

"Um," my eyes close but I can't think as soft lips press lightly over my inner thigh. "Uh... I'm thinking that fate is an asshole to mark me with a man who has so much hate and so little brains."

A grunt hums over my flesh as sharp teeth nip at my thigh.

A shiver tumbles all through me.

"You think I hate you?" Prey's breath is hot against my center as he talks low and menacing. I smile as I realize he's ignoring the low blow in that description of himself. "Hate fucking is best kind, Pretty Human," he whispers as his fingers trace back and forth along the apex of my thighs.

My legs shake but I try to keep my composure.

Every good vampire movie needs a little hate fucking...

My head lifts and Aston still watches me. He's inched toward the bottom of the stairs though, and he's just about to leave.

He should leave.

He should.

"You like him," My Prince whispers with that nagging curiosity in his tone. "Mmm he's uncomfortable. Make him more comfortable, Miss Vega."

My heart pounds to tell Aston to leave. To save whatever good image he has of me in his mind.

I shouldn't fuck Prey.

But so much of me wants him. Even if I know he'll never want me back.

I just want to know what it feels like. With the mate I'll never truly have.

Just once.

A hot mouth presses over my wetness and with one big swipe of his tongue he covers me fully. His hands hold my legs open hard and his mouth devours me even harder.

A gasp tears from my throat and still I cling to that pained hooded look in Aston's emerald eyes. Energy tangles through me with every swirl of Prey's cruel tongue. Too many sensations climb inside, settling low in my core. Breathless moans are all I have. As I watch Aston, I see that same erotic neediness within him.

Because he feels so much. He feels so much of me.

I want him to feel more.

"Aston," I moan, my head falling back but I keep gazing into the sensuality shining in the depths of his eyes.

At the sound of another man's name on my lips, Prey thrusts two fingers in hard. He arches them deep and grinds into me in just that one spot of pure intensity.

"Look at me," Prey growls as he fucks me harder with his hand, making me insane with every small move he makes.

Pain and pleasure shake through me as my spine arches hard, my attention struggling to do what Prey asked. He leans over me, putting even more pressure against my sex as he works me faster and faster. His hand wraps around my neck and he pulls me up despite the bow of my body. His lips hover over mine as he speaks.

"You're fucking mine. Your slick pussy," his fingers press harder against that perfect spot, "your moans and screams, and your fucking orgasm, are all mine." And with a slam of his lips and a thrust of his hand my sex clenches around him. All those reckless emotions crash down on me in a rain of euphoria trembling all through my body.

"Fuck, fuck, fuck," I whisper against his lips as he flicks his tongue against my curses before his teeth dragging over my lower lip.

And he bites there hard before sucking sweetly. Warmth trickles down my chin but I'm oblivious to anything other than the feel of his bliss washing into me. Magic bright and white lights me up. It tingles all through me and he pulls back before it fully settles low in my core.

"You'll always be the one I can't have, Pretty Human," he whispers against my lips. "Luckily for me, I don't want you."

He pulls his hand away, leaving me confused and with a new emptiness between my thighs where he once was. My Prince sits lazily on top of Pavel's croft, munching... is that popcorn?

I blink at the room and find the spot where Aston watched me from across the room. Except he's gone now.

Because I chose a man who will never want me.

Despite what fate may claim.

A heavy thought of embarrassment fills my chest but I shove it all away. I stomp it. And then I look up at the vampire storming away from me.

With a haze of blood red mist, I'm in front of him. I flurry in with sparkling magic drifting around my hair and eyes as I stare up at the arrogant asshole.

"Fuck your mark, Prey. And fuck you too." My chin lifts. I still want him.

The push and pull between us is electric and sparking and the hate he wears for me, it just makes all that needy energy burn up when we're near.

"Don't claim me." I lean in close to him, nerves firing through me with the brush of our hair as I whisper along his ear. "Spend the rest of your miserable fucking life without feeling the ecstasy a mate can bring you." My lips press to his cheek with a sweet fuck-you kiss goodbye.

But his hand snaps around my jaw before I can pull away. Sparking energy strikes between us. His other hand grips my thigh and he lifts me without warning. My back slams to the wall and his hips press into me nicely. He weights me against the brick and his head buries in my neck as he grinds into me slowly at first.

It's a twist of consciousness, it seems. He starts so slow. But with a grunt of power and dominance, he shoves down his jeans and slams into my wetness so hard my gasp is a soft, empty shriek.

"Fucking ecstasy huh?" He fucks me so hard the brick wall scrapes against my shoulders. His hand never leaves my throat and still he slams into me over and over again, using me and hurting me so much it's good.

His teeth drag over my neck but it's like he refuses to give me the release his bite might bring to me.

"It feel good yet? When's it supposed to feel good for me?" He insults me as he spreads my thighs further apart. His fingers dig in on either side of my wind pipe. His growl is a low violent sound along my shoulder.

My nails sink into the back of his neck as he slides in so deep, pain stings ever so slightly among so much tangling pleasure.

"Prey," I gasp, my thighs tightening around him as his thrusts grow reckless and wild.

"Fuck," he hisses as I cling to him harder. "Fucking human. Fucking beautiful human. Fucking," he breaths me in and his hips slow, his cock sliding against my sex with more affection than violence. "Fucking mate," he whispers against my neck as his hands both settle low on my ass and his rhythm is an intense grinding that I hope never stops. "Why did you have to mark on me, my Pretty Human?" He leans his temple against mine as his mouth parts wide without words.

He holds my gaze as we both gasp against each other.

He builds so much energy between us with just the depth of his gaze. The rocking of his hips pushes deeper. Deeper. So fucking deep until...

My nails drag down his shoulders hard as my screams cry into the crook of his neck as he holds me and lets me fall apart in his arms with shattering colors falling behind tightly clenched eyes. I shake and tremble while he thrusts in slower and slower before he stiffens in my arms with an endless groan.

As the magic sizzles like tingling numbness along my flesh, I realize we haven't kissed since the demon first commanded us to. It wasn't affection or love like Vuitton had described.

It was just fucking.

My mate claimed me. On my birthday even...

Why do I suddenly wish he hadn't?

We're a heap of shaking breaths and hesitant looks out of the corner of our eyes. The way he looks at me from my hair to my mouth and everything in between, I know.

Despite how hard my heart's pounding just for him.

I know he'll always hate me.

Maybe they all will.

But I'll be here anyway.

Fucking up their lives even more.

Until I get exactly what I want.

Revenge.

EPILOGUE

RIVAL

Pain like I don't remember in the last several centuries burns through my shoulders and back. My head lulls but when my eyes open, only gritty dirt across old stone flooring is all I see. I shift but my hands stay tightly in place above my head. The chains clash as I fling my head violently up to see what's holding me bound.

"Ruddy cunt," I hiss out with a mixture of raw anger and slicing pain.

They're out there rejoicing with a killer in disguise and they don't even know it. They locked me away and have just written off the threat who I know is watching their every move.

They're wrong.

Zavia's wrong.

And more importantly, Kira's wrong.

Blood trickles down my temple and over my jaw.

I never would have killed Kyra.

No more than I could have killed Kira.

Kyra was my responsibility. She asked for my help and I gave it.

And Kira...

She—she's my biggest threat. She could get me killed like I've seen so many before me die swift and fast.

All because they thought with their heart instead of their fucking brain.

My lashes fall and I spot the new mark just beneath the heavy lines of familar tattoos. A red splatter of a letter just beneath the old tattoos can be almost seen. Her letter.

It's such an enchanting mark of magic that it set my heart on fire since the moment it appeared. The moment I laid eyes on her in that shitty little apartment, it burned into me like an awakening.

Now I'm hers.

The blood splatter K imprinted on my chest says it all.

And I'll reject that secret until the day I die.

Thank you so much for taking a chance on my enemy lovers supernatural series. Book two, *Heartless Monsters*, continues with all the love

and hate and everything in between for Kira and her men.

Take a look at Heartless Monsters <u>HERE</u>!

If you want more updates on Kira and the men we love to hate join my Newsletter or Facebook Reader Group!
AK Koonce Newsletter
AK Koonce Facebook Group

ALSO BY A.K. KOONCE

Hopeless Sacrifice

The Secrets of Shifters

The Darkest Wolves

The Sweetest Lies

The Royal Harem Series

The Hundred Year Curse

The Curse of the Sea

The Legend of the Cursed Princess

The Severed Souls Series

Darkness Rising

Darkness Consuming

Darkness Colliding

The Huntress Series

An Assassin's Death

An Assassin's Deception

An Assassin's Destiny

The Monsters and Miseries Series

Hellish Fae

Sinless Demons

Dr. Hyde's Prison for the Rare

Escaping Hallow Hill Academy

Surviving Hallow Hill Academy

Paranormal Romance Books

The Cursed Kingdoms Series

The Cruel FAe King

The Cursed Fae King

The Crowned Fae Queen

The Twisted Crown Series

The Shadow Fae

The Iron Fae

The Midnight Monsters Series

Fate of the Hybrid, Prequel

To Save a Vampire, Book one

To Love a Vampire, Book two

To Kill a Vampire, Book three

Stand Alone Contemporary Romance

Hate Me Like You Do

ABOUT THE AUTHOR

A.K. Koonce is a USA Today bestselling author. She's a mom by day and a fantasy and paranormal romance writer by night. She keeps her fantastical stories in her mind on an endless loop while she tries her best to focus on her actual life and not that of the spectacular, but demanding, fictional characters who always fill her thoughts.

Printed in Great Britain
by Amazon

11104098R00109